THE LOST FRENCHMAN

Cully Long

SINGLE
ATOM
BOOKS

ISBN 978-0-9973488-1-1

www.SingleAtomBooks.com

CHAPTER ONE

The car ground to a stop, skidding a bit in the loose gravel of the shoulder and sending a cloud of dust and grit into the sky behind. She clawed at the seatbelt with one hand, and the door latch with the other, desperate to release herself from the metal container. Finally free, she ran into the Arizona desert and pitched forward onto her knees emptying her stomach into the red sand.

"Great. Perfect. Good work, Mallory," she muttered to herself scrubbing her sleeve across her mouth trying to remove the slick of saliva and sick on her chin. "You're really making some great life choices today." She looked back down the stretch of cracked blacktop road towards the Reservation and the place where she'd most likely just destroyed her career. Considering what had just happened, she expected there to be smoke and flames. Shouldn't there be some outward signs when someone's entire future is destroyed? Instead there was a cloudless, blue sky and a warm desert breeze that smelled faintly of flowers. She retched again.

This summer was supposed to jumpstart her whole life and set her up for a great senior year. When she'd informed her thesis advisors at the University of North Carolina that she had been granted an internship with Dr. Jonathan Toller on his upcoming dig in Arizona, they'd been overjoyed. She was a second year graduate student and Dr. Toller was one of the leading experts on the topic of the native populations of the Southwest. This dig was to be his crowning achievement and

Mallory Campbell would be there. One of their students would be part of the team!

The excavation had been talked about in academic circles for months; every student who knew how to hold a trowel was trying to get signed on to it and even some professors were agreeing to low-level positions on the dig, just to bask in the reflected glory of it. Naturally, Mallory's professors celebrated the announcement that she had been offered a spot as if she had been named expedition leader instead of just a lowly intern.

Mallory tried to hide it, but she really was excited by the job. It was going to be one of the most important expeditions in recent history: the expedition of a lifetime. After a decade of negotiations, Toller had been given permission to enter a section of the Kaibab Indian Reservation that had never been excavated or explored by archeologists; some of the approved areas of the site had not been seen by anyone outside the tribe since the founding of the reservation in 1934.

Toller's initial scouting trips had given him evidence that the site was a major trading post between two groups of Anasazi known as the Kayenta Anasazi and the Virgin Anasazi. Archaeologists had argued for decades, if not a century, as to whether these two populations were in fact one group or two, and if they were two different populations, which came first? Was one an offshoot of the other? Did the culture of the Kayenta influence the Virgin, or vice versa? In Toller's opinion, this site would answer those questions and probably many more, and though he had never said as much out loud, it was clear to Mallory that he also expected this site to confirm his personal theory: The Virgin were the originators of the local culture, and the Kayenta had appropriated it. If he could prove that, then he'd solidify his place in the pantheon of great American archaeologists and as the foremost living expert on the Anasazi. If the discoveries really broke his way, he could potentially become the American Howard Carter: the man who made an unknowable and mysterious culture familiar to the world.

2

This summer was also to be Mallory's first professional experience in the field. She had expected to be a "shovel bum:" the lowest menial labor on any archaeological site. She thought that she'd perhaps get to wash a few artifacts towards the end of her time, and she would have considered herself very lucky. Instead, she was shocked to find herself directly alongside Toller nearly every day working the most important sections of the dig.

She was shocked back to the present by the sound, somewhere behind her, of her cell phone ringing. It was back in the car, and she stood up and stared toward it wondering if Toller had already contacted her thesis advisors. She hadn't been off the reservation for that long, and Toller must have had more important issues to deal with than her, right? Was Toller mad enough or vindictive enough to have called them already? She wasn't sure.

Her thoughts strayed back to the past few weeks. At first it was hard not to be overwhelmed by The Jonathan Toller. Besides the obvious honor of working with him, he was charming. He had a boyish, "aw-shucks" sort of charm that made him seem surprised by his own fame and high position. It was made even worse by the fact that he was handsome. His face was sun-weathered and smoothed by the desert wind into the perfectly stereotyped ruggedness of an outdoorsman and he had a very carefully chosen look to remind anyone he met just who he was. He always wore a fedora with the perfect patina of age, just like Indiana Jones, and a denim chambray shirt with a red neckerchief like Alan Grant from *Jurassic Park*. He had cultivated just the right amount of silver-flecked beard stubble and he turned up the cuffs on his sleeves by exactly the right number of turns to accentuate his arms. The whole image screamed, "I am a handsome but respected scientist who works with his hands."

On the first day, Toller had gathered everyone on site in a small tent and delivered a stirring pep talk. Afterwards, while they had filled out paperwork, he had strode the aisles stopping here and there to speak quietly with certain staff members. She looked up to smile nervously as he passed her, and he stopped and came back to her side. He dropped into a squat beside her chair and peered at the form she was filling out.

"Mallory Campbell. Where have you been assigned, Ms. Campbell?" His voice was buttery and he annunciated each syllable with the practiced ease of someone who spoke to people for a living.

"I haven't yet," she replied.

"Good. Come to the main trailer when you arrive tomorrow. You'll be with me." He patted her knee good-naturedly and stood.

From that day forward, Toller had wanted her beside him every time he went into the field; she was there every time someone brought him a pot or tool that had been discovered. He often even asked her opinions of the pieces and made a special effort to make sure she held them and examined them. It was hard not to be flattered by all the attention, and she felt like she was being given very private access to the site.

She shook her head at the memory of it. She was tempted to be angry at herself for having been so excited about the assignment. After all, wasn't that why she was there?

She reached the car and checked the phone: Joyce, one of the few friends she had made on the dig. She slammed the car door and threw the vehicle into drive, pulling back onto the road without bothering to check her mirrors. Joyce would have to live with the mystery of where Mallory was for a while.

When most little girls were still hoping to add "ballerina" or "princess" to their future resumes, Mallory had already decided that she would be an archaeologist. Her room was like a mini-Museum of Natural History filled with the treasures that she had collected on her family's horse farm: Civil War musket balls and gun flints, clay pipe heads, drilled shells, arrow heads, pieces of porcelain dolls, and old bottles, not to mention the bones, feathers, and shells, or the mounds of quartz she had found.

She could look back and see the single moment when her life path became clear. She was 8 years old. Her father had been digging a posthole for a new fence while she sat to the side "sifting" the red clay in case there were any interesting "artifacts" buried there. Most days it yielded a few cool rocks, but that day she pulled a small, red lump from the pile of dirt that her father generated. It was about the size of a teacup, but she could see a smooth whitish surface exposed under one side. Together, she and her father had carefully washed and cleaned it, watching in amazement as the red clay melted away in the water revealing a tiny clay jar in the shape of a deer head.

Though it delayed completing the fence by several months, her father encouraged her to contact the local university. No one had expected the jar to amount to much of anything. Her father had thought it was probably a piece of a toy, maybe 50 or 60 years old, but certainly no more. In the end it turned out to be an animal effigy jar, a product of the local Pisgah tribe, and over 700 years old.

The students from the university had spent the summer excavating that corner of the pasture and checking for further artifacts. Mallory had spent the summer helping. Though the small dig revealed no further artifacts, her small jar now held pride of place in the North Carolina Museum of Art, and archaeology held a place in Mallory's heart. It had been the single most exciting thing that had ever happened to her. Rediscovering lost history seemed like the most interesting job in the world to her, and time had done nothing to change that.

It took an hour for her to get back to the housing for the dig site crew but less than 20 minutes to collect her belongings and get back on the road. She wanted to be long gone before anyone back at the dig really started asking questions. She'd called in sick the previous two days, so most of them would probably assume that she was still feeling ill. The ones who hadn't witnessed her flame out this morning anyway.

She figured that Toller had two ways to go with this: he could call her professors and tell them some story about why she had been dismissed, or he could ignore her and allow her own embarrassment to keep her silent when she returned to school. Calling anyone risked her contradicting his story. He was most likely counting on her keeping quiet, assuming that she would cover up her dismissal herself in order to maintain her position at UNC. If she went back to UNC and talked, it would be her story against his, and she knew who would win that war.

Her stomach churned at the prospect of dealing with this. Her career was likely at an end before it had even properly begun. There were four weeks until she was supposed to be back in North Carolina. That meant she had four weeks to figure out how she was going to fix this. How she was going to fix her life.

When she reached Highway 389, she sat at the intersection for an hour while all of her anger drained away and was replaced by sadness. This was the first choice of her new life. A right turn would take her to Interstate 15 and eventually Las Vegas. A left turn would join 89 and take her into the Utah wilderness. She looked down at the cell phone in the passenger seat. After Joyce, no one else had called. It felt like an act of cowardice to just turn the phone off, but if she could legitimately say that she had no reception...

She turned left and drove into the desert, trying not to dwell on what had happened. Her resolve lasted about a mile.

It had taken her nearly two weeks to put together what was really going on with Toller and why he constantly wanted her by his side.

The first thing she had noticed was that Toller only really "worked" in the dig units when the documentarians with their cameras were nearby. He was also most likely to take time to explain things to her when the cameras were nearby, and as soon as they stepped away, his explanations would end.

Toller finally showed his true colors toward the end of her third week. He had been working in a unit with another girl, a young co-ed who looked like a frumpy small town librarian, when the documentary crew arrived. Toller quickly ushered the girl out of the unit and asked Mallory to join him instead. As she climbed in she heard him say to the photographer, "Much better scenery for you now, eh?" followed by a broad wink. Just before the camera rolled he had leaned toward her and whispered, "You'll do great in this business, you know? The pretty ones always have an easier time getting shows on the National Geographic Channel."

He had then patted her on the behind.

Mallory's heart sank, and she was left with a sour taste in her mouth whenever she saw him, knowing that he only really wanted her there because she was eye candy for the cameras. Not to mention for Toller himself. His charm suddenly seemed like a sinister mask.

Mallory asked to be reassigned, saying that she really wanted to have the experience of seeing a unit of the dig through from start to finish, rather than hopping from site to site. The site supervisor warned her that Toller wouldn't be happy but gave her a segment of the gridded site to dig on her own, promising her that she'd be allowed to see it through.

Then came "The Incident," as she had come to think of it. She had been given a segment at the edge of the settlement in a residential section far removed from the kiva that represented the cultural center of the site. In Anasazi cultures, the kiva was a combination of a church and a city hall and, on most sites, the kiva was where you wanted to be. It was certainly where Toller was focusing his efforts. Her segment was the equivalent of being told to dig in someone's back yard, and someone unimportant at that. Her chances of finding anything worthwhile were extremely low.

The site supervisor had given her instructions to dig to a depth of 60 centimeters. Below that depth and they'd be so far back in history that neither the Virgin nor the Kayenta were thought to have existed as an organized culture. The 60-centimeter dig took her nearly two weeks and was *not* exciting. After 3 days, at a depth of 15 centimeters, she had found the

7

bones of a bobcat. At 20, she had found a layer of charcoal, which was momentarily exciting, but when she reported it to the site supervisors, she was told that it was expected and had been found in most of the grid sections in that area. At 26 centimeters, she found a piece of rock that she thought for a bit was the head of an ax. She was later told that it was not. After that, she found literally nothing, not even a particularly interesting rock.

She was mostly alone at her unit, though a few people joined her now and then including the frumpy librarian whose name, Mallory discovered, was Joyce. Most of them stayed in her boring little unit for a few hours, never returning after their breaks. Joyce lasted two whole days, but even though they worked well together and bonded over the job, she too found more interesting work elsewhere and didn't return for a third.

Alone in her unit, the digging became so monotonous and mind numbing that she ended up digging to a depth of 64 centimeters, mainly because she was on autopilot and determined to complete the assignment she had been given despite the uselessness of it. At 64 centimeters she found the thing that would eventually get her fired.

When she brushed away the dust at the edge of it, her breath went out of her. There in the dirt was the white edge of a piece of pottery. Her heart raced, and she felt just like she had as a little girl revealing the head of the deer underneath the cake of red clay. Sure, it was a piece of pottery, probably just like a million other pieces of pottery, but it was *her* piece. She spent the day meticulously uncovering it and photographing every millimeter of dust that came away from every possible angle with both her personal smartphone camera and the field camera she had been given. In the end, she had revealed a palm-sized piece of a pot covered in black and white geometric shapes.

She called the field supervisor to her unit. He jumped into the square area she had dug away and looked closely at the potsherd. "This is below the level you were asked to excavate to," he said, a note of reprimand in his voice. "But... nice work. You did a nice job with your edges; everything looks clean. I'll get a team over here to document it. You go over to..." he consulted a pocket notebook and picked out a new unit for her to begin work on. It was a clear dismissal, and he was sending her to another unit on the edge of the settlement, but she went to it with a smile and a feeling of triumph despite his unceremonious reception of her find.

The next day she walked past the unit where she had found the sherd and was surprised to find that it had been backfilled. Other than a little loose dirt, there was no sign that she had ever been there at all. She was even more surprised to find that the forward edge of the grid had been pulled back six meters. The unit was no longer even inside the approved area of the dig. When she tracked down the supervisor and asked about it, he had simply shrugged and apologetically mumbled something about the parameters of the dig having changed. "Time constraints," he said, "not much of interest out there anyway."

Her new unit was now outside the parameters as well, and she was reassigned again. This time she found herself doing exactly the tasks she had initially expected.

First, it was piloting drones over the site to photograph the landscape then spending hours at a computer digitally stitching those photos together so that someone else could look them over in hope of spotting a foundation, trench, or wall that wasn't immediately visible from the ground. It took days, and she never went into the field, instead spending her time hunched at computer. She consoled herself by thinking that she had at least learned a little bit about drones. Of course, she wasn't sure it was knowledge she'd ever get to use again, but knowledge is knowledge.

When that was done, she was told to report to one of the open-sided tents where students were washing artifacts. To her surprise, Joyce was there.

"Why are you here?" she whispered conspiratorially, slipping into a chair beside her and taking up one of the artifacts that needed cleaning.

"I've been doing scut for days," Joyce shrugged, "I had been doing cataloging but I showed up on Monday and they sent me over here."

"What? You're *way* better than artifact washing. You should have your own units."

"Says the girl who used to have her own unit..." Joyce replied in a gossipy whisper.

"Yeah, well... at least I know why *I'm* here."

"What? Why!?" she leaned in and listened to the story of the sherd Mallory had found. When Mallory was through Joyce leaned back with a smug look on her face. "I think I know what's going on." She motioned for Mallory to come closer and lowered her voice, "I was examining and cataloging pottery fragments that day. Toller came into the lab trailer and bumped a sherd to the front of the line. He didn't give me an item number for it, and when I asked how to mark it on the paperwork, he told me not to worry about it. He stood there and watched every move I made. He wouldn't leave the lab until it was done and, when he left, he took the sherd with him."

"And?" Mallory said, nearly breathless. She looked up to see if anyone else was paying attention to them. They weren't. Dropping her voice she asked again, "And? Was it Virgin or Kayenta?"

"It was Kayenta." Joyce said matter-of-factly. "No doubt. Virgin pottery used a sandstone mix. You can see the crystals in the clay matrix. Kayenta used a totally different mix."

Together they put the final pieces in place: the fragment had been found at the deepest level that anyone on site had excavated to. Mallory had most likely discovered the oldest piece of pottery that the site had yielded, and it was not from the Virgin peoples. The Kayenta predated the Virgin, and Mallory's sherd proved it.

"Wait right here," Joyce said and excused herself from the conversation. Mallory watched from a gap in the tent as Joyce stalked across the site, headed to the lab where undergraduates were cataloguing the artifacts and where Joyce had been working until just recently.

She was inside the lab for a nerve-rackingly long time. When she emerged, she made a straight line back to the tent. She returned to Mallory's side and picked up a piece of pottery, carefully washing it. When she was sure no one was listening, she whispered, "It wasn't cataloged."

"What? What do you mean?"

"I looked in every catalog we have, digital or paper. I even looked at the backlog of material. There's nothing. There's no record of your sherd. Not a paper trail. Not the photographs. Not even the equipment logs for the tools you signed out. There's not even a record of your *unit*."

Mallory slumped in her folding chair. Her stomach was at her feet.

"Toller's wrong. His hypothesis about the Kayenta, and maybe even this whole site, is wrong, and your sherd proves it," Joyce whispered harshly.

Mallory gulped air.

"He – he's going to cover it up. He's going to lie!" Mallory said, the realization dawning on her.

"It looks that way," Joyce agreed, "and we're the only ones who know."

CHAPTER TWO

When Mallory was twelve, she'd had an enormous fight with her best friend. It was the cataclysmic, world ending type of fight that can only really happen between two twelve-year-old girls. She couldn't even recall the root cause of the fight now, but she had a distinct memory of her father's advice for her.

She had spent days sitting on the wooden fence that surrounded the horse paddock, watching the young mares stroll about and sulking. On the third day, her father had taken a seat beside her and put his arm around her.

"What's going on, Mal?" he'd asked softly. "You seem low the past few days."

She collapsed into his side, a well of tears finally overflowing, and told him the story in a gush of words and tears, while he patiently listened. When she'd finished, he wiped the tears off her cheeks and said, "Mal, you just need to do one right thing."

"What thing?" she had asked, between hiccups of crying.

"Well now, I don't know the answer to that," he said. "Only you can answer that. But here's the thing: you don't have to fix the entire problem at once. You just have to find one right thing to do. And after that, find another right thing. And another. Soon enough you'll have fixed the whole problem. But start with the one right thing. You got it?"

"Yes, Daddy," she'd said, and hugged him.

"When you know what the one right thing is, you go do it. But don't go until you're sure," he'd said. "Once you know, once you are sure, you go and do it. See if it doesn't fix your problem."

Since that day, it has been a mantra for her. Whenever she faced a problem that felt overwhelming, it was the thing she focused on, finding the first step, the "one right thing."

After leaving the dig in Arizona, Mallory had driven up 89 until she passed through a tiny town called Memphis, Utah. She had spent many a summer weekend at horse shows in Memphis, Tennessee, and even though she was still 2,000 miles from home, seeing a familiar name was somehow a comfort. She turned in at a tiny motor court style hotel on the side of the highway. Two days passed, locked in the mangy little hotel room before her cellphone rang again. She had been in and out of service several times on the drive but was always surprised when there were no missed calls or messages. She pressed "IGNORE" on the screen, sending the call to voicemail. She pulled the ratty hotel blanket over her head and went back to her cocoon.

"I can't see the 'one right thing,' Daddy. I just don't see it yet," she muttered, and fell back into a dreamless sleep.

By the morning of the third day, she had fifteen missed calls. Some were from friends she had made on the dig, probably wondering where she had disappeared to, but some were from her thesis advisors and professors at UNC. Whether it was Toller or someone else who spread the story, it had obviously reached her advisors' ears.

The problem was that she was no closer to knowing what she would say to any of the callers. She'd made one attempt at fixing the problem, and it had blown up spectacularly. Since then she'd puked, she'd cried, she'd screamed, and she'd denied. She was rapidly approaching the point where the problem was going to outstrip her ability to do *anything*, and she knew it. Her stomach lurched again. She needed a distraction, and she needed it soon.

14

She had never been a drinker, or easily lost in television, or even a book. When she needed to distract herself, the best thing she had ever found was a long hike, and for years now, hiking had been connected to geocaching.

She reached for her iPad and with a few taps, she had the local cache map open. The map had a few icons peppered across it, most of them close to town. With over 2 million geocaches in the world, there were very few places one could go and not find at least a few. Most of the caches near her seemed to be pretty generic; the type of thing that was often dismissively referred to as a "park and grab." Most of them would require less than ten minutes of walking. That wasn't going to distract her for very long, if at all.

She expanded the area of the map and started looking at some of the caches that were further from town. She was drawn to a Letterboxing Hybrid Cache icon that was several miles into the local desert. She had a soft spot for Letterbox Hybrid Caches. It wasn't a common type of geocache. They were based on the older game of Letterboxing that had been going on since the late 1800s. Rather than using a GPS to guide someone to the final location, like a traditional geocache, it typically used riddles in the form of a poem to lead people to the treasure. It was quaint and appealed to her sense of history. This cache appeared to be the longest hike of any of the local caches, at least of the ones that didn't require a four-wheel drive to access. It would be the perfect distraction.

She read the description of the geocache from the website:

The Lost Frenchman's Letterbox
Letterbox Hyrbid Cache by Hoodoo Hiker
Difficulty: 2
Terrain: 3.5

Geocache Description:
In the late 1890's, a French homesteader and miner named Jean Tevbaugh came into a tavern at a settlement near here.

In his possession was a piece of deer hide with a map inscribed on it, a piece of quartz attached to a tin plate, a rosary, and a large spool of twine. Earlier that night, he had been seen in a saloon nearby bragging about a treasure that he had found and hidden in the wilderness nearby. According to witnesses, he had several nuggets of gold with him, which were described as being "the size of walnuts." It is said that he repeatedly told the other people in the tavern, "No one will find my treasure until they've prayed to three goddesses for help."

Over the years since then, the legend of the "Lost Frenchman's Mine" has grown. No one is sure what Tevbaugh found. Some say it was a vein of gold, some say it was an abandoned mine, or a cache of gold left by another prospector or perhaps a local Native American population. Some say it was a lost Anasazi dwelling or even El Dorado. Hundreds of people have looked for Tevbaugh's gold, some have even died for it, but no one has found it.

In honor of the Lost Frenchman, I have placed this letterbox in an area called "Three Goddess Canyons," where Milk Creek exits the canyon and starts its flow towards Colorado. Once you are in the slot canyons, GPS will be useless which is why I chose a Letterbox format. Park at the coordinates and follow the "Maiden Canyon Trailhead" north until you arrive at the mouth of three parallel slot canyons. This hike is about two miles. At the canyons, follow the clues in this poem to get you to the cache. It will be about another mile of hiking.

Maiden's Canyon to the west
Your canyoneering she will test.

Mother's Canyon at the center
You can't see the sky after you enter.

The Crone's canyon to east

It isn't deep and the path's a beast.

By name the water should be bright white
But it merely sparkles in the light.
Follow north the water's flow
Choose a canyon in which to go.

A canyon dry will make you whine
You will not get a log to sign.

Follow through climb and turn
If a reward you wish to earn.

Once the way's completely blocked
Look for a hole shaped like a box.

It will be a bit high up the wall
Stand on a rock if you aren't tall.

Once the log you've signed and stamped
Enjoy the canyon through which you've tramped.

* * *

She threw the small daypack that contained her geocaching gear into the back seat of the car and pointed the car towards the edge of town. As she drove into the desert, her phone rang three more times, which only resulted in her pressing the gas a bit harder. She knew that if she could get far enough out of town, she'd lose cell signal again and at the parking area for the trailhead, she had one bar. By the time she was 100 feet up the trail, she had none. She felt the weight of the past few days lift. She may not have a solution to her problem, but she had now put it out of reach. She couldn't deal with the problem because she had no access to it. For now, all she cared about was the beauty of the desert around her and signing a geocache log.

Three hours later, she stood on a tiny rock ledge over 10 feet above the sandy floor of a Utah slot canyon. The three-inch ledge barely had space for the toes of her boots and shifting positions was difficult as there was nowhere else to stand, but she needed a different angle of attack. The wax-slick brass tube in her hand scraped the walls of the sandstone hole where it was wedged, sending a stream of sand and grit showering down on Mallory's head. Blowing dust out of her face, she flicked her head to toss the sweat dampened auburn hair out of her eyes. She tightened her grip on the rock protrusion that was under her other hand, and strained to look into the cavity at the short tube of metal buried deep in the sandstone wall. No matter how she twisted it or repositioned it, she could not figure out a way to retrieve it. The problem was that the hole was above her head and just at the edge of her reach. She thought that if she could push the tube upward slightly she might be able to change the angle of it and slide it free, but her arm was already painfully extended, and she couldn't see past the tube to see what the shape of the little crevice was. She allowed the tube to settle and rested her forehead against the cool sandstone.

A plan came to her, but it was a bit on the crazy side and amounted to the same plan that a ten year old has when they need to retrieve a box of cereal from atop the refrigerator. Except she was more likely to break a leg.

With a shake of her shoulders, she let her daypack slide off and fall to the soft, wet sand below. She then unzipped her fleece and shook her arms free letting the fleece drift down to the canyon floor as well. As unencumbered as she could manage, she reached back into the hole, sliding her fingers beneath the tube and lifting it rather than gripping it. She slowly raised it, feeling it slide against the wall. Suddenly, she felt it tip back slightly. There must be a perpendicular opening somewhere in the dark recess that she couldn't see. Balancing

18

the tube on the very tip of her fingers, she slowly inched her hand forward allowing it to simultaneously fall back a bit into the cavity. Once she reached the maximum extension of her arm, the reckless part of the plan came into effect. She took a deep breath and counted slowly to herself... one... two... three... and leapt!

The action pushed the tube upwards. Simultaneously, she jerked her arm towards the opening counting on the friction of her fingertips to drag the tube forward as well, just like a kid trying to retrieve a cereal box that they can't grasp but can drag by their fingertips until it falls. She felt her fingertips lose the tenuous grip they had on the tube and hoped that she hadn't just sent it tumbling backwards into the rock wall where it would be lost, probably forever.

She couldn't worry about the tube right now though; she had other worries, like a vertical leap on a three-inch ledge that left her unbalanced high above the ground. Her left toe hit the slim rock shelf first and skidded on the gritty surface. Her right foot hit, and this time she felt the thick lugs of tread on her hiking boot grip the surface. At the last second, her hand gripped the edge of the hole she had just been reaching into and the muscles in her forearm tightened, pulling her against the wall, keeping her from tumbling backward into space. In her peripheral vision, she caught sight of the brass tube falling past her, and heard it land in the sand with a loud "chuff."

An electric tingle ran up her spine at the triumph, and she pumped her free fist, once. She exhaled slowly, until her lungs were empty, in an effort to calm the adrenaline now coursing through her and began to climb down.

Back on the ground, she retrieved the cylinder and dropped heavily onto a boulder, legs shaking from the exertion of standing on her toes for the past hour.

She turned the brass tube over in her hands. It was about the length and thickness of her forearm, capped at both ends and sealed with a hard wax. The wax was dark and pitted with a patina of age, some sand and stone embedded in the surface where she had scraped it against the walls. It had an ineffable air of antiquity about it, though there were no markings or anything to indicate an origin or age. Whatever this thing was, it clearly wasn't a geocache.

Mallory knew that geocachers often found things that they hadn't intended, including rare archeological items. Just months before, a cacher had found a rifle leaning against a tree in the Northern Utah wilderness. The old Winchester appeared to have been leaning there for nearly 150 years before the cacher found it. South of her current position, in Arizona, a cacher had found an intact Yavapai Indian jar that was estimated to be 600 years old. Had she accidentally found something similar?

The geocacher in her wanted to pull out a multi-tool and pry it open, but the archaeologist in her held back. This area had seen waves of settlers, homesteaders, and pioneers, from the Native American populations, to Mormons, gold hunters, and miners. There were over a dozen native populations who had lived in these canyons, not to mention the Spanish, Mexicans, Chinese railroad workers... the population and ownership of the land around her had changed so many times that almost anyone could have left this behind, or lost it, at any point in the last 400 years or more. The tube looked like a document tube, completely sealed at one end, with a cap fitted over the other and a slathering wax over the cap, sealing it as well. It weighed a pound or two but not much more. She really couldn't guess what it was.

She rolled the tube across her palm thoughtfully. Opening it in a lab would mean controlled conditions where she could contain any pollen or hair or other materials that she could use to date it. She'd need to clean it up, and photograph it, maybe x-ray the contents before opening. On the other hand, she'd already broken protocol by failing to photograph it in situ. Maybe she should just put it back where she found it. It wasn't a geocache and so wasn't her business.

She laughed at herself for even debating it. The chances were very high that she wasn't even an archaeologist anymore.

She may not even be a student. She'd crossed one of the most important people in her field and spent several days ignoring her thesis advisors. She shook her head in an attempt to clear away the worrisome thoughts.

She pulled out her phone; she still didn't have service, which only served to make her feel better. She'd saved the cache description in anticipation of losing service, so she was still able to reread the poem that had led her here.

The fifth stanza said, *"Follow north the water's flow/ Choose a canyon in which to go."*

At the mouth of the canyons, it had been very clear which canyon had a creek flowing through it. Crone's Canyon had been nothing but a dry arroyo, and while the sand in Mother's Canyon had looked damp and muddy in spots, there was a strong flow from Maiden's.

Of that canyon the poem had said *"Your canyoneering she will test,"* and Maiden's had tested her, as promised, with car sized boulders to climb over and sections of canyon that were barely two feet wide. The poem had said that *"Once the way's completely blocked/ Look for a hole shaped like a box."* Here at the end, where an enormous chockstone had blocked her way, there was only one hole in the wall, but it was round, not "box shaped," and there weren't any convenient rocks to stand on. In her haste, had she chosen the wrong canyon? She may not have an obvious choice on what to do about the tube, but she could backtrack and check the other canyon while she considered it. There was plenty of daylight left.

She slid the tube into her pack, delaying a decision, and returned to the canyon mouth. Even after completing the arduous journey a second time, she was still anxious to figure out what she had done wrong. A short hike into Crone's Canyon confirmed that it was not the correct choice. She found it blocked after only a few hundred feet. A huge tangle of debris and stone stood nearly thirty feet high, probably a deposit from a flash flood. There was no cache to be found here. She backed out and looked at Mother's. The sandy floor was damp and muddy. Water had flowed here in the very recent past. Could a rockslide or a flash flood have altered the flow of Milk Creek and shunted it to the western canyon? She took a deep pull from a water bottle and began her third canyon hike of the day. Here, the way was flat and smooth. Though she had to hop over a few muddy patches, the hike was no more difficult than a stroll down a gravel path.

A half an hour later, she found herself in a wide semicircular opening with large stones littering the edges. The back wall of the canyon tightened to a spare six inches wide. It would be impossible to pass through. She could go no further. She looked around at the canyon walls and found dozens of holes, both small and large, that had been worn into the walls over the passing centuries by water and wind, but one stood out: a near perfect rectangle the size of a shoebox. It was almost as if it had been purposefully cut in that shape, and just below it was a boulder. The excitement of the find took over, and she quickly jumped up onto the stone and reached into the "box shaped" hole, finding the hard smooth plastic of an otter box. When she pulled it out it was clearly emblazoned with a green geocache sticker. She'd found the cache!

She took a few minutes to sign the logbook found inside the cache, flipping through the names of some of the past finders: DavBex, PinkieTow, RaggedyAnimal, 52FarmAlls. These were the members of the secret society of geocachers, those few who knew of the treasures that were hidden all around the world and who had shared in sitting in this place and holding this box. This was one of her favorite parts of geocaching.

After logging the find and replacing the box where she found it, she made her way back to her car feeling the tired pull of muscle that marked a good day of hiking. A long drive later, and she was back at the rundown motel where she pulled out her iPad and completed the last step of a geocache adventure: logging the find on the website. She paused for a moment to consider how much she should divulge in the log, then set about writing.

Found it!
Geocache Log by: Catawba Girl

This was quite the day! I loved the hike. I haven't had an opportunity to explore very many slot canyons, and here I got a look at three! Had a little trouble with the directions at first. I think the situation on site may have changed recently, making the instructions no longer relevant. The CO might want to check on it. Once I figured out what I was meant to do, I easily had the cache in hand, not to mention a completely different "cache" that I'm still not sure what to make of. Tomorrow, it's back to the highway for the next leg of my vacation, but for today it's a well-earned beer and a night's rest. TFTC!

Just seconds later, her email program chimed, indicating a new email. She clicked over to it, and scanned the list of unopened emails. How many of her advisors had tried emailing since she had stopped answering her phone? There were a handful of the standard marketing emails, mixed with Twitter and Facebook notifications, and she counted seven messages with subject lines that led her to believe they'd be about the situation in Arizona. The most recent message, however, was from the geocaching website. The owner of the cache she had logged just minutes before had sent her a message.

From: HoodooHiker@email.net
To: theCatawbaGirl@email.net
Subject: [GEO] HoodooHiker contacting Catwaba Girl

Hey! I'm really intrigued by your log on my Letterbox Cache. I run a little backcountry supply company called Hoodoo Hiking Outfitters, at Main and 100 West. You probably passed it on the way out of town. We open at 9 a.m. I'd love it if you stopped by and told me a little bit more about your adventure!
Hope to see you in the morning,
Hoodoo

Putting aside the iPad, she pulled the brass tube from her pack and placed it reverentially on the chipped Formica table. She folded her hands on the table edge and rested her chin on them, eyes level with the cylinder.

"What are you?" she whispered.

CHAPTER THREE

Sitting in her small car in the parking lot of Hoodoo Hiking Outfitters, Mallory stared at her phone. She slid her finger across the screen, flipping through the gallery of photos that she had taken of the potsherd as she had uncovered it. Since returning to "civilization" after her hike, she had not received any new calls. She guessed that her advisors had given up on her at this point. It was so much easier just to ignore them for now. She knew that eventually she'd have to talk to them about what had gone down with Toller, but she simply wasn't ready. Her fear of losing her position had cooled, and now she felt only a deep resolution to fix the problem. Somehow.

"One right thing," she muttered and sipped at a cup of watery coffee. A faded red pickup truck moved through town, stopping briefly at a light, then continuing down the sleepy street. At this time of morning, at this season, most of the town was still shuttered and asleep. The only other person she'd seen so far had been the attendant at the gas station where she'd stopped for the coffee.

A white Toyota 4Runner, covered in red dust, turned off the street and maneuvered into an alley between the storefronts, bumping over the curb. A tall man unfolded himself from the truck and came around to the sidewalk where he casually unlocked the front door of the business and reached inside to flip an unseen bank of switches. The lighted sign bloomed into life, and the fluorescents inside flickered into existence. A tie-dyed t-shirt and baggy cargo shorts hung loosely from his bean-pole frame. His sun-bleached hair, in tight ring curls that would've made Shirley Temple jealous, was shoved under a worn bucket hat and below that a thick beard that obscured his face. She guessed that he was 40-ish, maybe 45? Though he was thin, his arms and legs were taut strands of muscle, and she thought that he must be a rock climber accustomed to days spent hanging from canyon walls. She wondered if he called himself 'HoodooHiker' because he looked like the tall, thin spires of rock that were his namesake or because he enjoyed hiking amongst the locally ubiquitous formations.

He stepped inside and flipped the sign on the door from 'CLOSED' to 'OPEN.' He stuck his head out of the door and looked towards her car expectantly. After a moment, his beard split into a beaming smile and he raised a thin arm to gesture in her direction letting her know that she was welcome to come into the shop.

Inside, she found the shop itself crowded and small, with backpacking, hiking, rock climbing, and canyoneering equipment covering every surface, even to the point of having spools of climbing rope hanging from the ceiling. Somehow though, it felt welcoming rather than claustrophobic. Trying to keep any tentativeness out of her voice she said, "I'm looking for... HoodooHiker?" Up close, she could now see that his t-shirt read 'Keep Calm and Belay On,' beneath a drawing of a carabineer.

"That's me!" he beamed and extended his calloused hand. She could feel the strength of his grip, carefully measured to be firm, but not painful. She thought that he was probably able to crush stone with those hands. "Carey Estes to the government, but everyone else just calls me Hoodoo. Are you Catawba Girl?"

"Mallory Campbell," she said, returning his handshake, trying to keep her own grip firm.

"You had a little trouble at my cache yesterday?"

She explained the problems she'd had while he busied himself booting a computer, counting out a cash drawer, and getting himself ready to open for business. He asked the occasional question or dropped the random "hmmm," into the conversation.

"Yeah," he said finally, "sounds like the creek might have jumped its bank and switched canyons. It happens. There was a big rain last month that might have caused it. You had a cryptic line in there about finding another cache? You didn't find the Frenchman's treasure did you?" he joked in a lilting Southwestern drawl.

"I did find... something," she quipped, and he looked at her quizzically. She had stared at the brass tube all night and still hadn't quite decided what to do about it. It was currently in her daypack, sitting on the floor between her feet, unopened and unaltered. She didn't want to talk about the tube yet, so she tried to shift the conversation back to him. "Did the Frenchman really hide something in those canyons?"

Hoodoo derisively snorted and said, "I doubt it. Not those canyons anyway. What do you know about Tevbaugh?"

"Tevbaugh is the Frenchman's real name? Nothing I guess. Just what you had on the cache page," she answered.

"Oh, then let me spin you a yarn. Grab that stool," he said, indicating a rickety collection of sticks at the end of his counter. While she moved it, he withdrew a rolled paper from a cubby beside him. He took on the air of a lecturer, a practiced speaker who was used to relaying information to other people. She wondered how many tourists he had told this story over the years.

"To begin with, like a lot of local legends, Jean Tevbaugh may or may not have even existed, but it is true that there used to be a mining town just north of here. If you know where to look, you can still find a few remnants of it: foundations and chimneys and the like. It's also true that the hills hereabouts are full of secrets: old mines, caves, settlements, all kinds of stuff. Some say that the Anasazi and

Freemont peoples may have left behind whole cities that haven't seen a human in a century or more. There's just too much land out there, and all the canyons and mesas that rise up out of it are just too hard to map and navigate." He quirked up a corner of his mouth and shrugged.

"Anyway," he continued, "the story goes that ol'Tevbaugh found something out there. Something potentially valuable the way it's told. He'd disappear out into the wilderness for weeks at a time, and sometimes come back with a nugget of gold, or piece of silver and turquoise jewelry, or the like, sell it and then go back out there. Legends say that the last time he came out of the wilderness, he was real excited about his latest find. He spent the whole night at a bar telling everyone who would listen that whatever it was that he had found was going to set him up for the rest of his life."

"Now, legends disagree here," he continued. "Some say he was killed, some say he simply died in his sleep, and a few say he disappeared into thin air, but all the stories agree that no one ever saw him alive again after that night. They found his body in the local hotel, along with a few weird things. I honestly think that the stuff they found is the thing that makes people so fascinated with this legend."

"What stuff?"

"Well. The map of course. The original was burned into buckskin and rolled up in a copper tube."

Mallory felt her heart quicken. "C-copper?" she asked.

Hoodoo shrugged, "Copper, brass, lead. I'm not sure. I've even heard gold from some. He also had a big ball of twine, nothing really special about that. There was a rosary, which was a little more unusual. Utah has never really been a hotbed of Catholicism. The really weird thing though, the thing that most of the treasure hunters focus on was the quartz."

"Quartz?"

"Yeah. The legends get really tangled up about this one. The only thing they agree on was that there was a piece of quartz, attached to a sheet of tin somehow." He held his palms up and the corner of his mouth quirked.

"I don't get it," Mallory said.

"No one does really. Miners did all sorts of crazy stuff. Dowsing. Ley lines. Pendulums. Talismans. If they thought it would lead them to gold, they did it. Most people assume it was some kind of magic thing. Maybe he looked through the crystal? Who knows."

"What did it look like?" she asked.

"No idea. The best description I ever heard was a metal sheet, about the size of a paperback, with a piece of quartz attached in the center."

She contemplated it for a moment, and asked, "What happened to all that stuff?"

"Oh, long gone. Every once in a while a treasure hunter will turn up with a piece of quartz strapped to a metal sheet, swearing that it's the real deal, but they never seem to be able to prove it or make much out of it. But... we have the map."

He tapped the rolled scroll of paper he had pulled out, then slowly unfurled it. On the poster sized paper was a series of rough scribbles that looked like a kindergartner's idea of a treasure map. A sinuous dashed line zigzagged across the page, passing childish drawings of a house, a ladder, a heart, a deer, and several other things. At the bottom was a series of 6 concentric shapes that were roughly semicircular with ends that went off the edge of the page.

Mallory looked at him, trying to mask her disbelief. "This? Is the map?"

He chuckled. "This is it! Well... not this. This is a poster. Every shop in town sells these, or replicas on leather. There are even a few shops that sell it as a cast concrete stone with the map carved into it. I have it on a t-shirt if you want one," he winked and gestured with a thumb at the wall of shirts behind him. "No? Your loss."

"And the original?"

"Who knows? Just like the quartz, it shows up every once in a while. Some treasure hunter or gullible tourist will stroll into town with what he claims is the gen-u-wine article. It'll have some scribble on it that this map doesn't. They never amount to much. But people still come every year to try and find the treasure." He shrugged dramatically, to punctuate the uselessness of it all. He had seemed animated and lively through most of the story, but suddenly a cloud had passed over him, and he looked momentarily lost in a melancholy, his attention focused elsewhere.

Mallory thought again about the tube she had in her pack. "Tevbaugh doesn't connect at all to the canyons where you hid your cache? It's called 'Three Goddess Canyon' and on the cache page, you said that his last words were —"

"It's a chicken or egg problem." He said snapping back to the present and cutting her off. "Yeah, his last words were 'To find my treasure you'll have to seek three goddesses,' or something like that anyway," he made a dismissive gesture with his hand, "Legends disagree, but as far as I can tell, that canyon system was called 'Willis Wash' in his time. I suspect that the... I don't know what to call it. The triple nature? Of the canyon led people to start calling it 'Three Goddess Canyon' after the Frenchman story got spread around. Everything around here has half a dozen names. What the Indians called it, what the Mormons called it, what the Bureau

30

of Land Management calls it," he snorted a breathy chuckle, clearly amused by it all. "It's a lot. Not to mention that every cowboy and miner had their own names for things so that they could discuss mines or good grazing land with their compatriots without people trying to jump the claim. I put my cache there because I like the story, and I like the canyon, and I thought people might enjoy the hike. No other reason."

"Ah," she mused, not entirely convinced by his dismissal. "You said treasure hunters come by here all the time. No one has ever found anything?"

"Oh... people claim they've found things all the time." He indicated the map, "It doesn't look like much, but there's just enough information on this map to get people into trouble. This knife for instance," he pointed at a crudely drawn thing that could be interpreted as a dagger. "It's been tied to a knife shaped hoodoo, a knife petroglyph on a canyon wall, and a little spring called Dagger Creek. Probably a dozen other places over the years. I could give you a list like that for every symbol on here. Every year someone will say they've made a connection that no one has ever thought of before. Who's to say who has the right of it?"

Mallory couldn't help herself. She was being drawn into the mystery of the treasure and the legends that surrounded it. She was fascinated. The archaeologist in her wanted to root out the truth of the story and find the artifacts associated with it. The geocacher in her wanted to find the treasure. "Is there anything everyone agrees on?" she asked eagerly.

"Oh yeah!" He reached up and tapped the button on a large flat screen television that was hanging beside him. It blinked into life and resolved into an Apple desktop. He reached under the counter and moved around a mouse that she couldn't see. On the screen, Google Earth bloomed into life; the familiar globe zooming automatically down to the corner where the shop was. "I use this to show backpackers good trails and backcountry landmarks," he explained. "Big screen is great for that!"

He manipulated the mouse, and the satellite imagery shifted north and west settling again on a desert wilderness where she saw a series of rock formations that she recognized as "fins," arched protrusions of rock that shot up out of the Earth, sometimes to heights of hundreds of feet, though their width fluctuated from 50 or 60 feet to less than a yard. Fins stacked side-by-side all through this area, with deep, rocky canyons between them. This series of fins looked like dinner plates stood on their edge in a dish drainer, arching up from the ground and back towards a mesa where the space between them diminished until they joined together again, forming the top of the mesa.

The mesa stood nearly alone, separated from the nearby plateau by what she guessed was at least a mile. She could see a dirt road that ringed the mesa, on the desert floor, but otherwise it looked completely desolate.

"This is Paradise Mesa," he said, indicating the flat area. "Over the years, pretty much all the treasure hunters have come to agree that the map points here."

"Why?" She asked, incredulously.

His finger dropped to the map and traced the sinuous line that crossed it. "This," he said, "is the only path that will get you up these." His other hand pointed at the fins on screen. "You start here." He pointed at the heart on the left edge of the map, then he turned to the screen and zoomed in to the bottom of a fin where the slickrock transitioned to the sandy desert floor. A small square appeared on the screen, indicating that someone had uploaded a photograph geotagged to that location. Hoodoo clicked on it, and an image of a rock wall with a pile of rubble at the bottom opened on the screen. At the top of the rockslide was an area that was clearly the source of the rubble: a piece of the wall had broken away and fallen, leaving a near perfect heart shape on the wall.

"Oh!" Mallory said, "Wow! That's amazing!"

Hoodoo smiled at her and continued. "If you go up the rim of this fin until you are able to cross over to the next, then down that one for a bit, and over to the next," as he described

32

it he traced the squiggle of line on the map with a forefinger, which roughly followed the up and down that he was describing. He continued, "You eventually find this." He clicked another photo icon and a wall of petroglyphs scraped into a mineral deposit known as desert varnish popped into view. In the center of the photo was the petroglyph of a deer. The deer on the map didn't match precisely, but it was close. "It continues like that until you reach the end. The trail leads you in a zigzag up and down the fins, and every icon drawn on this map has a match in the real world. No one's ever found a better path across the fins." His hand shifted over to a large circular drawing on the map that looked somewhat like a cartoonish eye, at the end of the path. "You finally end up here: Paradise Mesa."

"These circles represents Paradise Mesa? Why?" she asked, excitedly. Wordlessly, he shifted the image on the screen and zoomed out a bit. Mallory realized, for the first time, that the top of the mesa was roughly a circle, and just south of the center was a large dark patch, like a pupil in a cartoon eye. He looked at her to make sure she had made the connection, then he zoomed in on the dark spot.

"This is 'Frenchman's Eye.' It's... well... for lack of a better word, it's a hole. There's a spring at the top that eroded a pit straight down into the mesa. It's nearly 300 feet deep, and over three tenths of a mile wide. At the bottom is a whole ecosystem: trees, a stream, birds. You can't see it in satellite photos like this, but there's an old cabin down there too. Legend is that it was the Frenchman's cabin. People think this is where he went when he disappeared for months at a time."

"Holy cow!"

"Yeah. Problem is... you can't get there anymore. The path across the fins from the map is impossible now. The last fin, the one that should have connected to the mesa, is gone. It collapsed back in the nineteen-teens, and since that fin fell, the only way to the top of the mesa is rock climbing. As far as anyone can determine, the only way to *ever* get down to the cabin was rock climbing or repelling. Do you really think a 60 or 70 year old man repelled 300 feet down into a pit to hide?"

Mallory considered that. "Has it been explored?" she asked.

"Oh, heck yeah. Dozens of people have been down there. I outfitted a rock-climbing group myself, a couple years back. We even had a treasure hunter a few weeks ago, with more money than sense, who landed a helicopter on the mesa and sent drones down into the Eye."

"Ugh. Drones," she muttered, remembering her days of piloting them on the dig.

"He got chased off by the Bureau of Land Management and was arrested. Seems he broke a bunch of flight ordinances. Lucky someone called the BLM about it." He beamed a mischievous smile at her. "Anyway... yeah. It's been explored. I'm sure my..." he paused for a moment and looked momentarily wistful again, then continued, "I'm sure the first person to figure all this out was positive they were about to go home rich. So far, no one's turned up with any money though. At least no one who shared that news with the rest of the world."

She let that hang in the air between them for a moment and asked, "Do you believe there's really a treasure out there?"

He leaned on the back counter and crossed his arms. "I don't know." He sighed. "If there is, you'd need... Well. You'd need a lot more information to find it. This old map is like staring at clouds: you can make it mean anything you want. The lines could be roads or streams or canyons or trails. The shapes could represent rock formations, place names, rock carvings. You can see anything you want in the lines on this map." A deep frustration surfaced, making him sound almost angry about it all. "Yeah, it matches the trail on the fins, but some of the connections are a stretch at best, and if that trail is the correct interpretation... well... there's no treasure on top of that mesa."

"You sound sure of that," she said.

"It's been scoured clean," he said pursing his lips in an expression that showed no doubt. "Plus, there's just so much

34

about the story that doesn't make real sense. No one has ever come up with a good explanation for the other stuff Tevbaugh supposedly had with him when he died. I mean, a rosary is easy enough to explain, but that piece of quartz? What was that for? It doesn't even sound... real."

"Would you hunt for it?" Mallory asked, with a bit of a tease in her voice. He stood up and rolled up the map then pushed it back into the cubby.

"I have." He sounded tired and bitter. "I've worked in this shop since I was 24. That's nearly 20 years of outfitting treasure hunters. You don't do that without making an attempt for yourself now and then. I've heard all the theories and watched them all fail. Of course I've had a few theories of my own over the years." He winked slyly at her, showing a bit of the twinkle he'd had in his eye when she first entered the shop. "Every legend has some basis in truth, they say. Why not this one?"

"I have one more question," she said, "the copper tube that was in Tevbaugh's room: know anything about that?"

"Not a thing," he admitted. "It disappeared along with everything else."

Mallory's head was a flurry of thought and contradiction. The object in her bag could be anything: an artifact, a replica, a decoy, or something entirely unrelated to Jean Tevbaugh, the 'Lost Frenchman.' She'd never know until she opened it. A thought occurred to her. "You said Paradise Mesa was on BLM land, right?"

"Yep."

"So... why do people look for the treasure? Other than... what? Bragging rights? They'll get nothing out of it. The government owns the land. That means the government owns the treasure."

"Ha! This is treasure hunting, not an old man with a metal detector at the beach. Treasure hunters can be a rough crowd. They aren't exactly the type that run down to the county to get an excavation permit. If there's something out there they want..." He shrugged.

"What about you? What if you found the treasure?"

"Me?" his features glazed and his eyes drifted to the map on the counter. "I'd like to know what's out there. I think the mystery is what matters to me. The secret." He smiled. "Not to say I wouldn't mind picking up a couple bucks..."

She laughed. She thought that his answer was probably the same thing she would have said if someone had asked her that question. "Then I guess it's my turn to tell you the rest of my story." She reached down and pulled her own tube from her pack, dropping it onto the wooden counter between them with a satisfyingly noisy "clunk."

Hoodoo's drowsy blue eyes lingered on the tube for a few heartbeats then rose to meet hers. She said, "I found this at the end of Maiden's Canyon. I thought it was the geocache at first."

He raised a hand as if to touch the tube, then withdrew it. "You're yanking my chain right? This is what you found?"

"Yeah. Now that I've heard your story I can see how... weird it is... but I really did find this yesterday," she said, with a bit of embarrassment in her voice.

He stared at her, then it, then her, letting more than a minute pass. "Have you opened it?"

"No," she chuckled lightly, "my... training... has stopped me so far." That was all he needed to know right now. "But after your story, I think... I mean... do you think? Maybe?"

"Training?" he asked, turning his back to rummage through a series of drawers in the counter behind him.

"I was an archaeology grad student. I mean, I *am* a grad student. If my professors ever found out that I found a sealed container that is potentially 100 to 150 years old and I didn't open it in a lab, they'd kill me." She fought a blush that she felt rising on her cheeks. Of the list of things that she hoped her professors didn't know about, this tube was actually pretty low.

"Well. They can't kill me," he replied and brandished a multi-tool that he had pulled from the drawer. "Can *I* open it?"

Mallory's eyes widened. This was the end of her indecision, one way or the other. By revealing the tube to a second person she had taken the decision away from just herself, but there was no turning back now. Since finding the brass tube, she'd begun thinking of herself as a rogue archaeologist: the rule breaker that dug too deep and removed artifacts from their places, the student who mouthed off to the most important person she'd ever met. This though? This was what drove her, what had always driven her: the need to know, to uncover the hidden truth. When she was confronted with a mystery, she did everything she could to solve it. It's what made her a good archaeologist and a good geocacher. Maybe it would make her a good treasure hunter too? She felt like she was standing on the edge of something. Whether that was a cliff, or a new path, she wasn't certain, but if she was going rogue, she might as well go all the way.

She nodded once, firmly. "Do it. Let's see what's in there."

CHAPTER FOUR

The tiny shop reeked of WD-40 and beeswax. It had taken Mallory and Hoodoo two hours of elbow grease, a knife, a paint scraper, a can of WD-40, and finally two strap wrenches to remove the hardened wax and pry the cap off of the tube. It now lay on the counter between them.

"Should we...?" Hoodoo asked, a quiet reverence in his voice.

"Yeah. Yeah... Yes." Mallory stammered, "Just give me a second to..."

"Of course! Take your time. You found it, you should..."

She took a breath and counted to three, then reached out and lifted the tube, upending it slightly, and reached in with her index finger. Her eyes widened and she looked up, meeting Hoodoo's eyes.

"What?" he asked.

She slowly drew her finger out, pulling a rolled piece of leather from the tube, thin as a chamois. The outside of the rolled leather was still covered in short, soft fur, pale brown, with white spots like a fawn's hide. She laid the leather onto the counter reverentially, and it unfurled a bit, revealing some dark markings on the inside.

"No way. No way!" Hoodoo breathed. He walked away from the counter with both hands tugging at fistfuls of his curly hair. She watched him pace a small circuit through the crowded store.

"What is it?" she finally asked. He stomped back to the counter.

"You're setting me up, right? This is a prank. Or... or a scam! Is this where you offer to sell me your miraculous map?" A note of anger had started to creep into his voice, just at the edge. The laid back drowsiness that had been in his eyes was gone, replaced with a penetrating sharpness, the ice-chip blue threatening to burn her.

"What? No. No! I promise. I don't... I don't know what this is, or where it came from, but... I... everything I told you was true. I found it. It was in the canyon. I... I don't know anything else." She glared at him.

He sighed. "I'm sorry. You just have to see it from my side. I put out a cache about the legend of the Lost Frenchman who, by the way, kind of casts a long shadow around here, the cache is in an area that really has nothing to do with the Frenchman, then you show up with... something... I'm just suddenly having a hard time accepting..."

"Hoodoo... Carey," she said, invoking his real name for the first time, "I can only tell you that I find this as weird and unbelievable as you. Trust me?"

He stared at her for a long moment then nodded curtly. "Okay'" he said, voice still hard. "Then let's see what we have." He reached down and gently unrolled the piece of fawn leather between them. Despite its apparent age, it was still supple and unrolled smoothly. He moved a coffee mug full of ink pens that was near the register, and he placed it onto the edge of the leather to hold down the heavily curled edge. They both stared at the exposed side and the series of marks and drawings that covered it. The markings seemed to have been burned into the leather, leaving an indelible mark.

Across the top edge were six 'V' shapes, arranged in two groups of three, with a space between them: VVV   VVV

Below that was a three lobed shape that could represent a leaf or a tulip or a flower of some kind. Maybe it was a

40

sassafras leaf? Did sassafras grow out here? She wasn't sure. There was a black dot at the "heel" of the shape and another in the rightmost lobe. Bracketing the shape on either side was a straight line, about 6 inches on one side, slightly shorter on the other.

Below that, the leather sheet was dominated by three figures drawn in the style of a Native American petroglyph. The three figures had triangular upper bodies and appeared to be holding hands. The left figure had a circular shape behind its head that looked like the sun or a halo. The central figure, which was a bit larger than the other two, had what could be multiple arms, and the third had a spiral beside it that could be a wheel or perhaps a tail.

The rest was nearly covered by large block printing in five lines of lines of text:

THREE GODDESSES LED ME HERE
TO FOLLOW YOU MUST
PRAY TO THE MOTHER
SEE AS THE CAT
WEAVE AS THE SPIDER

Mallory slowly traced the edge of the leather with her finger, then lightly touched the curve of the 'R' in 'SPIDER.' She quietly breathed, "what?" She picked up the tube and upended it then peered into its depth. There was nothing else there. The only thing that fell out were a few stray hairs that had separated from the leather.

She looked at Hoodoo who reverentially fingered the row of 'V's at the top. "I think..." he said, and turned to pull out one of the rolled posters. He shifted the leather to make space on the counter and unrolled it. He slid the edge of the leather onto the edge of the poster and slid it around for a few seconds, then pulled away the poster and dropped it on the floor without rerolling it. He dug in the cubbies for a moment and pulled out another rolled sheet. He unrolled that one and placed it under the leather where the other had been. Mallory could see that it was another poster of the Frenchman's map but at a different scale. He stopped and looked at her. "Do you remember me saying that I had my own theories about the Frenchman's map?" he asked.

She nodded.

"Well... no one has ever come up with a good explanation for these semicircles at the bottom. Some have said that they represent the sunrise or sunset, and that you should be reading the rest of the map while facing east or west, depending. Others have tied them to a canyon or a creek or a road... I've always thought that they weren't semicircles at all." He went back to the leather, sliding it back and forth. Finally Hoodoo lined up the 'V' shapes with the bottom of what had appeared to be concentric semicircles on the poster. Mallory instantly recognized that he had been right. They weren't semicircles. With the addition of the 'V' shapes it became clear what they were: nested crescent moons. The 'V's completed the shapes, forming the points of the crescents.

He quietly said, "I've never told anyone that theory, and I've never heard anyone else say that they thought it might be the case. There was no way that you could have known."

"What are you saying?" Mallory asked.

"I'm saying that I not only believe your story... I think I believe that this might be the real thing," he answered. "I think you found a piece of the Frenchman's map."

Suddenly, he was a flurry of activity: pulling bundles of coiled rope from the ceiling, packs from shelves, compression bags full of stuff from under the counter, and tossing them into a pile in the center of the floor. He stopped and spun to face her. "What are you doing?" he asked, incredulously.

"Me?" she answered.

"Yes! Get your packs! You need a change of clothes, maybe two. What kind of camping stuff do you have with you? Do you have a sleeping bag? No? It's okay... I have plenty." He grabbed a bag from a shelf and threw it with the other items at the middle of the room.

"Wait. Wait! Stop for just a second! What are you saying?" She grabbed his arm and stopped his frantic movement. He bit his lower lip and slowly turned his head to one side as if pondering who she was and how she had gotten there.

"I'm saying that I think the map is real. But more importantly... I know where to go. I know what the crescent moons mean." His eyebrows went up, asking the unspoken question. When she didn't respond he continued, "I just assumed you'd want to go too?"

Mallory's mouth slowly opened. Her head was a buzz of thoughts competing for attention: her professors, equipment she had on hand, the possibility of finding something, being in the desert alone with a stranger, the possibility of *not* finding something, Dr. Toller, sleeping overnight in the strange environment, were there rattlesnakes? Scorpions? This man was a stranger. Could she go out into the desert with a stranger?

Before she could answer any of those questions, the bell on the door jangled and a woman entered.

Hoodoo greeted her with a huge smile, "Babe! Just in time. Can you watch the store today? Mallory wants to go out to Paradise Mesa." He looked at Mallory and noticed a look of confusion on her face. "Oh! Mallory, I'd like you to meet my wife, Lynn."

The pretty blonde woman extended a hand, "Pleasure to meet you," she said, "I was just bringing Carey some lunch, but I guess I have good timing." She was a warm and welcoming woman, with lightly tanned skin and a golden sheen to her hair that indicated she must spend as much time out in the sun as her husband. A twinkle in her soft brown eyes echoed the smile on her face. Though she was pretty, if Mallory had been asked to describe her, she thought the first word she might use would be 'tough.'

"It was his idea. Really!" Mallory protested.

Lynn laughed. "Yeah. I thought as much." She went up on her tiptoes and kissed Hoodoo on the cheek. "He'll go out to that mesa any chance he gets. The least excuse sends him running to his truck. Don't worry about it."

"You don't mind him leaving you to run the store?" Mallory asked. With surprise, she registered that she had made a decision about whether she was going with him. Not really knowing why, something about this woman's entrance had made Hoodoo seem... safer? She wasn't sure that was the right word but something had changed.

"Oh, did he give you the idea that he was some poor, put-upon shopkeep? He might share a nickname with the store," Lynn leaned over conspiratorially and whispered "but I own it." Mallory looked at Hoodoo with an expression of "Oh?"

He rolled his eyes a bit and said, "Her father founded the store, but he left it to *us* when he died. I may not be a 'put-upon shopkeep,' but I am her business partner." He pulled his wife into an embrace and kissed her lightly.

Lynn looked up into his eyes and asked, "How long will you be out there this time?"

"It depends on what we find today." Hoodoo responded. "Young Mallory thinks she can find the Frenchman's treasure."

"Oh ho!" Lynn laughed. "Well... In that case..." She pulled an orange plastic device, about the size of deck of cards, from a drawer. "GPS doesn't work well out there. The fins and canyon walls just bounce the signal round. This is a satellite rescue unit. I try to get him to carry it whenever he goes out but he always seems to forget it."

44

"Having instant help is kind of against the point of going into the wilderness…" Hoodoo tried to interject.

Putting a hand on his forearm and raising her voice above his, Lynn continued, "When you settle in to camp, just press this button, and wait until the green light flashes. That will send me a message to let me know that everything okay. It will also attach your GPS coordinates to the message. If you have any trouble, and I mean *any* trouble, it's the same process, but you press this button instead." She indicated a button marked 'SOS.' "We have this device set up to deliver the message to my phone rather than rescue services or the company that makes the device. It will work even if there's no cell service where you are. If you get into trouble, don't let him talk you out of using it." She pressed the device into Mallory's hand.

Hoodoo turned his face to the ceiling as if seeking help from the heavens. He sighed deeply and said, "Go get your clothes and things, and I'll finish packing in here. Park your car behind the shop, it'll be fine back there." He went back to grabbing random things from shelves and boxes.

When Mallory had exited and closed the door Lynn turned to Hoodoo and said, "Was this really her idea?"

He shrugged. "Mostly," he lied.

Lynn shook her head in gentle mockery. "Have you told her about your Dad?" she asked.

"I told her that people have died on the trail," he admitted. "She doesn't need to know that my Dad was one of them." He reached under the counter and removed a worn and ragged leather notebook. He opened it to a page that had three concentric crescent moon shapes drawn in bold, sure strokes. "Look at this," he said, laying the open notebook beside the two maps, which were still arranged on the counter so that the crescent moons were formed. "My Dad was right, he just didn't have the rest of the information. If he'd had this…" he tapped the leather map with an index finger and the let the rest of the sentence die.

Lynn examined the two maps, leather and paper, and flipped through the notebook. Both of them had stared at these pages hundreds of times over the years, since it was found among his father's things, but neither had ever been able to put together most of the cryptic notes it contained. In its own way, the notebook was as enigmatic as the Frenchman's map. Hoodoo had added his own notations here and there, when information came to light, but it was still nothing more than scribbles and conjecture on most pages.

Lynn put her arms around his waist and looked into his eyes. "Just promise me you'll be careful. This might be the information your Dad was missing, but it might just be another blind alley."

"I know," he said. "And I promise. But you know why I have to take her out there, right?"

"I know," she said. She pecked his cheek, and then chose a selection of freeze-dried foods from the shelf and stacked them on the counter, waiting for him to pack them.

Outside, Mallory went to her car and started pulling items from the suitcases. Once she had what she wanted, she sat down on the hood, pulled out her cellphone, and made a call to her brother. It went to a voicemail, which she had expected. He should be in class at the moment. She knew that, unlike her mother or father, he'd take the message in stride and accept it at face value without overreacting. "Hey, it's Mal. I know mom and dad are probably looking for me. They've called a few times. There's some... stuff... going on out here, but I'm not ready to talk about it yet. Anyway. I'm about to do something that's either incredibly stupid or potentially brilliant. It involves being out of touch for a few more days. I'll try to check in, but I may not have cell service. If you haven't heard from me in... let's say 72 hours... then check my email. The password is the dog's name. Please don't make me regret telling you that. There'll be a photo in my email that has GPS data attached. Start looking for me there if you have to. I love you!"

She quickly snapped a photo of the front of the shop and emailed it to herself, then moved her car. Behind the shop, she took a minute to consider exactly what it was that she was doing. She pulled a notebook from the backseat and made a quick series of notes: Hoodoo's real name, the address of the store, some notes about the map, Paradise Mesa... everything she could think of that someone could use to find her if things went terribly wrong in the next few days. She folded the pages and wrote her brother's name on the front, as well as the word 'POLICE,' and left it on the passenger seat.

She locked her car and started her walk back to the storefront, then returned at the last moment and retrieved her caching daypack from the trunk. This was where she kept everything she needed for geocaching: her GPS, tools, spare batteries and anything else she'd ever needed while out on the trail. No point in going out unprepared. The Frenchman may not have ever envisioned GPS or satellites, but he had a geocacher's spirit, and she was ready to be "first to find" on his cache.

She went back into the store, failing to notice a faded red pickup idling at the intersection.

CHAPTER FIVE

Hoodoo drove like he was in a car chase on a 70s cop show. Mallory found herself reflexively pressing on the floor of the passenger seat, first with her right foot, then both, searching for the nonexistent brake.

In an effort to distract herself, she turned to face out the side window and watched the dry desert of Utah flash by. Long expanses of flat nothing were punctuated by the occasional rock formation that rose up from nowhere and then fell again. Sometimes they stood as lone sentinels looking out over their kingdoms of desert sage and tumbleweeds. Others stood in groups against wide mesas that dominated the sky for miles before abruptly ending and returning to flat, open expanse. She caught glimpses of arches, hoodoos, and other formations that stirred her explorer's heart. This certainly wasn't the Blue Ridge Mountains of her childhood.

"Crowing Rooster Mesa," Hoodoo intoned, indicating a rock formation to their right.

They passed the road to the trailhead that she had visited the day before, and she watched it flash past. What was the connection between those canyons and the Frenchman? Hoodoo insisted that he knew of no reason why the Frenchman would have hidden anything out there or who else may have been responsible for the map making its way there.

Had someone else stolen the map and hidden it there? Had it been misplaced somehow? It was likely they'd never know.

"Parliament," Hoodoo said, pointing to their left at a cluster of red hoodoo spires. He had been doing this periodically since they left Memphis, Utah an hour ago. Otherwise, he had been pretty quiet. She guessed that it was a mental tick leftover from working as a tour guide for so long. "Viewpoint Arch," he said, then suddenly, "hold on!"

He slowed a bit, but not much, and made a hard left. Other than a break in the roadside fence and a cattle grid set into the ground, Mallory could see little evidence that there was a road here.

"The rain last month left this road pretty washboarded," he said, "so it's going to be bumpy for a while."

Now that they were off the highway, Mallory could see the ochre-red strip of barren sand that he was charitably calling a "road." It stretched out in front of them for an indeterminable distance before curving around a large rock formation and disappearing. She could feel the vibration as the ruts under the tires of his old Toyota 4Runner beginning to shake the vehicle.

"How long is 'a while?'" she asked.

"About 20 miles. Don't worry, you'll only hate it for the first 10." He laughed. He had slowed after turning onto the dirt road, but it didn't feel like much of a change. The tiny ridges in the road couldn't have been more than half an inch deep. How could they shake the truck so violently? The large tires and raised suspension of the vehicle helped somewhat but not much. She thought if she had been in her own car, it would have started shedding parts within miles, shaken loose.

"P-p-p-pulpit R-r-r-rock," Hoodoo said, pointing forward, into the distance. He smiled at her and fell into silence for rest of the drive.

* * *

It took nearly two hours to cover what would have probably taken them 15 minutes on the open road, given the way Hoodoo drove. They slowly approached a large plateau that had grown to dominate the landscape. The ruffled edges, buttes, hoodoos, and fins that occasionally rose above the line of the main plateau created a riot of shapes that were like the skyline of a foreign city that begged to be explored.

Finally, Hoodoo slowed and appeared to be scanning the side of the dirt road for something. Apparently happy with what he found, he cautiously turned the vehicle off the road and bounced over a small ditch. She couldn't see much of a difference between the land he was driving over and the land they were passing, but she had to trust him. She thought that if she squinted a bit she might see the tracks of previous tire passage, but she wasn't sure.

"Paradise Mesa," Hoodoo said, pointing towards a large mesa that stood alone, apart from the wall of the main plateau.

"How do you know how to get there? There isn't much of a... road..." Mallory asked.

"Like I told you, I bring people out here all the time: treasure hunters, hikers, climbers, scout troops. I brought a watercolor painting group out here once," he shrugged. "It's less crowded than the national parks and has just as many great spots."

"Is it just a straight shot?"

"No... no. In fact..." He turned the truck towards the wall of the plateau. Paradise Mesa slipped to their left. In a few hundred feet, she started to see a change in the land. There was something in the middle ground between them and the plateau, and they seemed to be headed slightly downhill now. Soon, the details started to resolve themselves, and she could see that there was a canyon, or a wash, between them and the plateau.

"Are we going around that?" she asked.

"Nope," he answered. She could see now that the canyon was thirty or forty feet across. She couldn't make out a depth

51

yet, but it looked deep. "We'd need to go 20 more miles north before it would be shallow enough to cross, but that's pretty close to the plateau and there are some large rocks we'd need to dodge, and the desert floor is too uneven to drive on. We could have come off the main road before this canyon, but there are some areas that way that are pretty inhospitable too. Big ditches to cross, that sort of thing. The best way to get out there is to cross the Devil's Backbone." He indicated a formation that she would have called an arch if she was standing in the canyon, but from up here she'd call it a bridge.

He slowed to a stop and craned to see over the hood of the truck, carefully choosing the path onto the land bridge. The surface of the bridge was not flat; it sloped off to either side, making a roughly rounded shape. The truck slowly crept out onto the bridge, and she could now see that it was about fifty feet to the floor of the canyon from there. Her hand involuntarily crept up to the handle above the truck door, and she flashed on her brother calling it the "oh, crap handle" because the only reason you ever touched it was if you had just said, "oh, crap." Her other hand found the edge of the seat and tightened on it.

She could barely believe it possible but by the time they reached the center of the land bridge, it had narrowed even further. She could see no land beside the car when she looked out the window. She knew that if she opened the door at that moment and stepped out that she'd be stepping into empty space. It felt as if they were barely moving, and Hoodoo was practically standing up, hunched over the steering wheel in an attempt to navigate.

She heard a soft scrape on the bottom of the truck, the rocky surface of the bridge hitting the undercarriage. She let out a little squeak of terror and squeezed her eyes closed.

What felt like hours later, she heard Hoodoo let out a "Whoop!" and felt the truck accelerate. They had cleared the bridge. She opened her eyes and, realizing that she had been holding her breath, sucked in a lung-full of air.

"What. The. Hell?!" she screamed and swatted his chest with the back of her hand.

"Oh, come on!" he yelled back, "I've done that four or five dozen times! It's a great way to get your heart going!" He nearly giggled.

"I'm going out into the middle of nowhere with you. ALONE! I need to TRUST you and stunts like that-- with no warning! Are not the way to get me to do that!" she screeched at him.

He raised his eyebrows and nodded his head toward one shoulder saying, "Fair point. I promise to warn you next time." For the next half hour, she seethed in her seat watching the mesa grow in the windshield.

"How did you start geocaching?" Hoodoo asked, in an obvious effort to win her back over to his side.

She turned her head to him and repeated the story in a clipped voice, "I was working as an interpreter at a state park in South Dakota. Part of the arrangement was that I would live in a cabin on the parkland besides just working there. Most of my job was telling the visitors about an ongoing archeological dig and helping them understand what they were seeing." Despite herself, her voice had started to soften as she remembered her time at the park. "There was a lot to do during the day, but the evenings were pretty empty. I spent a lot of time reading by firelight. On my days off, I was really looking for something else. The park provided GPS units to visitors if they requested them. I thought that was pretty weird until one of the rangers described geocaching to me. Turns out, it combined everything I never knew I wanted combined: being outdoors, using technology, and finding hidden stuff. On my next day off, I borrowed one of the park's GPS units and used it to find my first cache. Three years later, and I have over 1,000 finds."

As she spoke, the mesa came to dominate the landscape, and the awe of the thing replaced what anger she still held. She could start to pick out some of the details that she had seen in the satellite image before. She could see fins rising from rubble and boulders to join the main body of the mesa, which was slick red rock that rose straight up from the desert floor. She could see that there would be no way to get to the top without climbing the face of the mesa. Or flying.

"The heart-shaped rockfall from the Frenchman's map is over that way," Hoodoo indicated and steered the opposite direction. "What we want is over here." He skirted around the mesa keeping it on the left of the truck until they had passed most of the large fins and were on the "back" side of the formation. He pulled into the shadow of a gigantic boulder and came to a halt, turning off the truck.

He hopped out and grabbed his pack from the back of the truck indicating that she should do the same. He had given her a lightweight hiking pack, larger than her normal daypack, which had an integrated water supply. He had provisioned it with things from the store, leaving room at the top for her to place her stuff-sacks of clothing and her caching bag inside. She hefted it onto her shoulders and adjusted the straps a bit, settling it into a comfortable position. She pulled her GPS receiver out of her pocket and allowed it to find her position on the globe then clipped it to her pack so that she'd have some sort of trail that she could download later. By the time she was ready, he was already a few hundred yards in front of her headed towards a ridge of rock that rose out of the ground like a ramp.

She turned in place, amazed at the oddity of the landscape. No matter how many times she travelled to this area, she was always amazed at the bizarre beauty of the desert and the thing she loved most of all was the constant changefulness of it. Even a short hike would take her through several kinds of landscape, from barren and rocky to lush and green and back again, all surrounded with towering rock formations and spires of precariously balanced stone. To one side was the watchful rise of the mesa, adding an anticipatory air to her surroundings. In the other direction was generally flat desert extending to the horizon. Out towards the direction she thought the road was in there was a small cloud of dust rising into the midday light. There must be another vehicle out here, perhaps an ATV or a group of four-wheel drive enthusiasts.

"Yo!" Hoodoo yelled from behind her. She turned and ran to catch up with him. When she reached him, he looked over his shoulder at her and said, "Tell me, young Mallory, have you ever hiked Angel's Landing in Zion?"

"Yeah, a couple summers ago." She responded, thinking back to the harrowing experience. The trail was only a half-mile long but it rapidly climbed several hundred feet to a pinnacle that overlooked a huge valley. The problem was that the trail wove back and forth over a razor thin fin of rock sometimes less than two feet wide and exceedingly steep. Some sections had chains to pull yourself up with, others relied on the hiker to figure it out and make their way as best they could. To either side of the trail was a drop to the valley floor, over 1,200 feet. A fall from the trail would be like diving from the side of the Empire State Building. She remembered being petrified at several places but determined to finish, mainly because there was a geocache at the end.

"Okay, good. Hidden Canyon?" he asked.

"Yes." It had been a similar hike with high narrow ledges that hugged rock faces but without as much height.

"The Subway?" he asked, continuing to plumb her hiking resume.

"Yeah. But I did that one with a professional guide who rented out the water gear. I didn't have that sort of stuff with me." That hike had required some swimming and minor rope climbing.

"Great. That tells me a lot about what you're capable of and what kind of experience you have. I think you'll do okay," he said.

"Now you tell me," she responded sarcastically. "How dangerous is this going to be?"

He shrugged. "You told me to warn you about things from here on out. Here's your warning: towards the end of the hike today we're going to cross a section that is very similar to Angel's Landing." He stopped and turned to look at her.

"Except there are no chains to hold on to. You think you'll be okay?"

She pursed her lips and cocked her head a bit. "Thank you. Yes, I'll be fine," she lied, determined not to show any weakness.

"Good!" he said. "Don't forget to drink your water," and with that, he focused on picking out the path that he was following up the fin.

The stone surface of the fin was steeply arched and worn smooth from wind and erosion. The lugs of her boots gripped the surface, but she still occasionally felt a foot slip. Before long, the fins on either side of them had risen higher than the one they were climbing, and the pink and white striated walls cast them into shadow. It felt like walking down a long wide hallway, with a really slanted floor.

Soon the walls lowered again, leaving them in the open air. The fin that they were on leveled off and they had a wide, flat surface to walk on, but she tried very hard not to notice that there was a drop of a few hundred feet on either side of them. Hoodoo periodically peered over the right edge and eventually sat down with his feet dangling. She caught up to him and looked over the side to see that there was a ledge about ten feet below them. It was narrow but slanted upward slightly, tipping toward the face of the stone they were standing on. He indicated downward with an index finger and, without saying anything else, slid off the edge of the fin. She heard his feet hit the ledge below them almost immediately.

She let out a slow breath and sat down. She looked over the edge at the ledge below her. Beyond it was an open gap, a space between the fin she was on and the next. She couldn't tell how deep it might be. Down the ledge, Hoodoo was staring up at her with a look of quiet anticipation. Her stomach flip-flopped in protest, but she took a quick breath and scooted forward, allowing gravity to pull her down. It felt like she was sliding for minutes before she hit the ledge, but she knew that to be a trick of her own anxiety. She took a deep breath to push away the anxiety and opened her eyes to find Hoodoo already turning and moving up the trail.

It continued in that manner for about an hour. They climbed short sections of rock then slid down others. Sometimes they were atop the fins, at other times they were between them, though they never seemed to go very far down towards the floor of the desert, staying instead towards the top of the fins. Hoodoo seemed to be following nothing more than instinct. Mallory had to concentrate on every step she took. The path was invisible until he had walked it. There were no trail markers or the small rock cairns that marked many of the desert trails she had been on. There didn't even seem to be a disturbance in the sand. Hoodoo moved like a cloud. He glided over the land, brushing past obstructions. Obstacles just didn't seem like obstacles to him. Mallory did her best to keep up, but it took her a lot more effort. She knew that the close walls of the fins meant that her GPS track wouldn't be very accurate, but she hoped it would be something at least. She had lost all sense of direction and place.

Finally, they emerged from a long tight section between two fins, and she found herself on a relatively wide, flat piece of land covered in fine sand with some low juniper and pinyon pine growing around the edges. Large walls stood on either side, giving her the sense that they had just walked out onto a stage and were about to be presented to an audience.

She inched forward to the edge of the "stage" and peered over. Below her was a long thin ridge of rock, an eroded and decayed fin that looked like a large staircase built from Legos by a three year old. It rose and fell in a jagged, unpredictable swoop that was roughly the shape of a cable on a suspension bridge. Just below her, it started a downward arc from the edge of the stage area and then back up to the top of a large pinnacle about a thousand feet away.

Hoodoo came to her side and pointed across the gap. "We need to be over there," he said.

"What? Is that, like... 'Three Crescent Point' or something?" she asked.

"Nah. Nothing back in here has a name. You might not have noticed but this isn't exactly an established hiking trail. We may be the only people to have stood at this point in," he paused dramatically, "maybe hundreds of years." He looked around as if taking in the grandeur of that moment, then his signature wide grin split his bushy beard. "Except, of course, for the fact that I've been out here myself a couple dozen times." He nudged her heavily with an elbow to punctuate his joke.

Mallory sniffed a short laugh. "Why is that, anyway?"

"Why do I come out here? Lots of reasons: climbing practice, solitude, the occasional treasure hunt." He smiled. "But really... I'm just drawn to this mesa. I've explored it as much as anybody I know of. I've even climbed down into the Frenchman's Eye a time or three. I found this place a couple years ago. There used to be this plein air painting group that I'd bring out here on excursions once or twice a year. I'd guide them to a nice viewpoint and set them up with tents and food. They'd paint for a couple days, and I'd... explore." He slid his pack off his back and removed a length of rope that had been clipped to the side then uncoiled it and looped it around a gnarled juniper at the edge of the flat area.

"We'll need to hand-line down to the first landing. It's pretty steep. Once we get out onto the ridge, I'll free climb and try to place lines for you but there may be some areas where that won't be possible. You ready?" he asked.

She shuffled closer to the edge of the outcropping and looked down. It was a bit more than ten feet down a steep rock face to a narrow landing. One either side of the landing, the rock dropped away steeply for several hundred feet. She already felt a panic welling in her stomach, but knew that she had to do it.

Turning back towards Hoodoo she caught a flash of white light, far below, like the sun glinting off of polished metal. She quickly looked back but saw nothing except rock and scrub grass. "Uhm. Yeah... let's do it before I lose my nerve."

CHAPTER SIX

Mallory stood at the halfway point on the ridge, one hand clinging to the twisted root of a long dead tree, the other clutching the rope that looped around a large boulder above her head. Hoodoo was on the next landing just above her, reaching down for her, if she could manage to reach that high.

Reaching the low point of the swoop on the ridge had taken all of her concentration and an enormous effort to tamp down her fear. She had tried to keep her attention focused only on the next step and what was in front of her, but she constantly felt like she had been about to fall forward and, therefore, off the ridge. Climbing down backwards with ropes and lines to support her felt safer, but that arrangement could only happen in certain sections.

She hoped that climbing up the other side would be easier because her sense of falling forward would mean that she was falling toward a rock face, not toward open air. But first she had to begin the upward portion of the climb. She pulled on the rope and on the root, pulling herself both upward and forward, and felt her weight shift from her lower foot to her higher foot, then she straightened and rose. Hoodoo helped her up another small rise, and she was standing on a small ledge with him.

"That's probably the hardest bit," he said. "That first rise is pretty steep. There's one more tricky bit of business up the way, but I'll explain it when we get there."

They continued for a few more minutes; Hoodoo seemed to effortlessly hop from rock to rock while Mallory had to use both her hands and her legs to control her ascent. She had been right that concentrating on the rock in front of her was easier, and she was barely aware of the drop on either side of her. Soon they came to a section where they were on a narrow ledge with a drop to the left and a high wall of stone to the right. She glanced ahead of them and saw that the ledge came to an abrupt end, terminating in a stone wall nearly as tall as her. At the top of the short section of wall was an ancient juniper whose roots stretched over the surface of the stone.

"This is it," Hoodoo said, "We need to get up there."

"It doesn't look so tricky," she said, craning to see what he may find so concerning.

"What you can't see is that there is a drop off on the other side of that stone. We need to use the tree to pull ourselves up. At the top, you need to turn your body to the right and go to the other side of the ridge. There's really nowhere at the top to pause or stop. You have to do it in one motion. That's important: one motion. I'll go first. Watch what I do. I'll help as much as I can from the other side," he said.

"Alright." She nodded, trying to sound braver than she was actually feeling.

"After this, it's basically a stroll out onto the pinnacle. I promise," he said. He ducked his head under a large root of the juniper and twisted his body. She knew that her smaller stature would make this more difficult for her. Then he reached up and grabbed the tree, pulling himself through the narrow opening between the root and the stone. She saw his face briefly as he turned his body and seemed to slide head first over the wall, disappearing. Seconds later, his head and shoulders appeared behind the tree; she could see that he was straining a bit to lift himself up. "Your turn!" he called, then dropped back down. "Don't stop!" she heard him yell from the other side.

She moved to the tree, turned her back to the stone wall, and reached up. Where his whole head and shoulders had been above the root, it fell in front of her eyes. She grabbed the root and hefted. Her feet were off the ground, and her arms were supporting her entire weight. She kicked her feet a bit, trying to find purchase on the stone face, and her right heel landed on something, a tiny ledge or protruding stone. Pushing against it added just enough to the strength of her arms that she was able to lift herself the rest of the way.

She found herself sitting on the edge of the wall. The wall was beneath the center of her thighs with the root at her knees. She immediately corrected her position, trying to tip forward so that her center of gravity was above the stone, but she made the terrible mistake of looking behind her. There was nothing. She saw only open sky and the rocky ground a million miles away. If her weight were to tip any further backwards, she would simply disappear.

"Here!" she heard Hoodoo bellow in her ear, and his calloused hand closed around her elbow and yanked her roughly towards him. There was a glimpse of sky, of tree and of rock and somehow, she was on her hands and knees on solid ground on the other side of the wall, Hoodoo sitting on his heels on front of her. "You alright?" he asked.

She took several deep breaths and lifted her face up, "Yeah. Thanks." She pulled herself into a seated position and took the water he was offering her. Her hands shook a bit, the sudden burst of adrenaline draining away and leaving her muscles weak and rubbery.

"It's over," he said, and pointed up the path. He had been right, there was maybe 20 feet left and the path was so flat and clear that it looked like a sidewalk.

"Okay. Just give me a minute," she replied. He sat down beside her and the looked out over the desert towards the huge plateau on the horizon. She scanned the view and noticed that the fin across from them had a huge arch at the upper edge. Despite the ubiquity of the rock formation in this region, they never failed to be impressive. This one stretched for a long distance, looking like an archer's bow left leaning against a wall. Out of the corner of her eye, she caught a glint of light.

"Did you see that?" she asked, pointing in the direction of the light.

"What?" Hoodoo asked, following her gaze.

"Something... I don't know. Like light glinting off a mirror or something. I saw the same thing when we were back on the other side before we crossed the ridge," she continued squinting in that direction, trying to catch it again.

"Yeah?" he shrugged. "Could be anything. Lots of campers, hikers, bikers, ATV riders... this desert isn't as unpopulated as it seems sometimes. Come on. I don't want to lose light before we have to go back across this ridge."

He stood and offered her a hand then pulled her upright. They strolled to the top of the pinnacle, all of Mallory's nerves and fright gone now. The ordeal lent her a feeling of immortality. She had faced death already today and beaten it back. Nothing else could happen to her.

The area atop the pinnacle was about the size of her bedroom back home, and the ground looked like a lump of used clay that had been discarded and left to dry in the sun. It had a whitish cast, unlike the reds, oranges, and pinks of the other stone around them. It sloped gently, but not enough that her footing didn't feel secure. One side of the formation was slightly higher with a pile of boulders that looked like another discarded lump of clay.

Hoodoo walked to the area beside the pile of stone and lay down on his stomach then motioned for her to join him. She walked over and lay down, only then realizing that the pile of stones formed a small arch! It was low to the ground, not much higher than a table, but with a long horizontal opening beneath. Hoodoo pointed through it and she saw that it aligned almost perfectly with the arch that she had seen earlier, out on the ridge.

"Oh! Two!" she exclaimed.

"Look again," he said. "Remember, there were three crescents on the map."

She squinted into the distance and realized that there was indeed a third arch beyond the one she had seen. Beside her, Hoodoo was extracting a pair of binoculars from his pack. He peered through, adjusting the focus and scanning a bit.

"Looking through all three... I don't know. It looks like there's a stone wall beyond them. I don't see anything special about it. I thought I'd see something, a clue, or... something. I don't know." He handed her the binoculars and rolled onto his back. "Okay, Tevbaugh. I'm here. What am I supposed to be seeing?"

Mallory looked through the binoculars for herself, moving her head back and forth, then up and down. "You can see quite a bit of that wall depending on the angle you are viewing from, but I still don't see anything remarkable." She turned to look at him. "I hate to ask, but... how sure are you that this is what the map is referring to? I mean... the shape of the arches isn't... as arched as the crescents on the map."

He rolled back onto his stomach. "I don't know. I was sure... until we got here. Now... I don't know. Let me look again." She handed him the binoculars, and he refocused on the wall. For twenty minutes, they alternated the binoculars between them, shuffling from side to side, looking from every extreme that allowed them to see through all three arches.

Beside her, Hoodoo pulled out an old leather bound notebook, creased and worn, and flipped through the pages. She could see a few cramped scribbles on the pages but nothing exciting. He kept the notebook angled away from her so she did what felt polite and pretended not to notice it.

Ultimately frustrated, Mallory started to push herself up and felt the heel of her hand slip a bit, sliding into a depression in the rock. She focused on it and then narrowed her eyes recognizing what the depression was. She began brushing small stones and sand out of the depression, defining it's edges and reassuring herself that it was what she thought it was. She wished she had the brushes and trowels she had used to excavate the potsherd in Arizona, but her fingers would have to do.

Finally satisfied that she had exposed enough of it, she pulled her phone from her pocket and clicked through to her photo album. She had the map in her pack, safe in its tube, but she had also extensively photographed it. There in her albums was a collection of photos of the map, right next to the collection of photos that she had taken of the fateful potsherd. She may not be able to protect that archaeological find, but she could protect the map and that started with not exposing it to the arid desert conditions if she didn't have to. She found the photo that she wanted and held it so that she could see both it and the depression. A smile spread across her face. Hoodoo who was still paging through the notebook, and she reached over, lightly hitting his side with the back of her hand.

"Hey. Hey! Look at this," she said. He rolled over and, seeing the expression on her face, sat up. He used his hand to shield the screen of the phone and recognized the three lobed shape that had been drawn beneath the crescents on the map. Then he looked at the ground. His mouth fell open.

"It's... a dinosaur track," he said.

Mallory continued brushing out dirt and pebbles, refining the edges and searching for the bottom of the track. It was very clearly defined and so sharp that she could start to see individual pads on the bottom of the foot. She thought that if she had a brush with her she might be able to clean the track to the point that she'd be able to see the ridges on the toes. It was as if the animal had tread in mud just yesterday. Soon her search yielded the fruit that she was actually looking for: a small round depression near the heel of the track. She shifted her attention to the right-most toe, hoping that there would be a second.

Hoodoo looked at the photo, then back at the track. "Is that hole you just uncovered the dot he has on the map?"

"Maybe," she said. "I hope so." As she said that, her finger found the second hole. "Yes! And here's the other one." When it was clean, she looked at him and said, "Now what?"

"I don't know, but I have a theory." He maneuvered his body a bit and lay down with his head near the track. "I think the holes are... sights. Like on a gun." He shifted and moved his head, trying to line up the two holes with the crescent arches. "Yes!" he exclaimed, "if you look down the imaginary line that connects the two holes, you are looking straight into the arches. Hand me the binoculars."

He lifted the glasses to his eyes and peered through for a long few moments, then looked above them, then back to the glasses.

"I still don't see anything," he said, a little exasperated.

Mallory, who had been studying the photo, asked, "What about these lines?" She showed him the phone, indicating the two lines drawn on either side of the track. The line to the right of the track was about the same length as the track, and the one on the left was about three quarters the size. They both stared at the phone for a few seconds, then Hoodoo stood up, "Wait," he said and ran down the path towards the tree where they had climbed over. She watched him pull himself up and snap a branch off of the tree, then run back.

"It's the straightest one I could see," he said, stripping the side branches and needles until he was left with a stick about eighteen inches long. "Let me see the map again." He compared the map to the track, and then laid the stick atop the track, as if he were measuring it. With a bit of effort, he snapped the stick so that it was the same length as the track, from heel to the center toe. "Maybe we're supposed to measure against the track, and maybe we're supposed to measure against the map. I'm not sure yet. But let's try the track first." Looking back at the photo, he estimated the relative length of the second line compared to the track and snapped the twig again. He was left with two sticks, one about 8 inches long, and the second about 6 inches.

He placed the longer stick into the hole near the heel of the track, and the shorter went into the hole in the toe. He asked, "Can you hold these please?" Mallory reached out and took the sticks, trying to hold them as straight as she could. He moved back and positioned himself so that he was looking down the sticks. Once or twice he reached out and adjusted the position of her hands, straightening the sticks, then adjusted the position of his head. Finally happy, he lifted the binoculars and sighted down the line. In this position, his head was lower than it had been before. The change in position also meant that the ground they were sitting on cut the first arch in the distance into a sliver of what it had been when his head was higher. He could barely see through all three arches now. Another minor adjustment, and he suddenly saw something. He shifted the focus knob a bit and brought the far wall into sharp focus.

"Well. I'll be..." he said, voice drifting away. He handed her the glasses and waved his hand in a gesture that she read as meaning that they should swap places. When she had settled in his position and adjusted the sticks as he had done, she lifted the binoculars.

She adjusted the focus so that the first arch was sharp, then the second, and finally the wall of the fin beyond them both. At first, she didn't see anything, but a slight shift of her shoulders revealed the secret. In the wall was a niche, a horizontal crevice that formed a shallow cave of sorts, where a piece of stone had long ago fallen away. At the back of the niche, she could barely make out something that looked like a low, curved wall made from mortared stone. It looked something like an old wishing well without the wooden roof.

"What is it?" she asked.

"I think it's a granary," Hoodoo replied. Noticing the question in her eyes he continued, "the Fremont People and the Anasazi both used them; they are little bricked in storage areas where they kept dried corn and beans. Most times, they are on cliff faces. If you aren't looking for them, they blend right in. I've heard of miners and homesteaders finding them and using them to stash equipment and things. Maybe Tevbaugh did that?"

She looked back into the binoculars at the strange little structure. "The real question," she asked, "is how do we get there?"

CHAPTER SEVEN

Hoodoo had worked for about an hour, sketching maps, profiles of rock formations, and other information into his battered notebook. Then he had poured over a compass and the topographic maps he had stored in his GPS. Meanwhile, Mallory had scoured the dinosaur track clean and photographed it from every angle. She wondered how many people beyond herself, Hoodoo, and Tevbaugh had ever been to the cap of this hoodoo and seen this remnant of life from 200 million years ago. Alone the track would have made everything she had faced on the hike worth it but it was also a new piece of a larger adventure and she couldn't help but think about what would come next.

The trip back across the spine of the ridge had been tiring but uneventful. Mallory wasn't sure if her experience on the way over had hardened her against being afraid of it, or if she was just distracted by thoughts of the granary and the other things they had discovered.

On the flat area that she had come to think of as "the stage," Hoodoo had produced a tiny black cylinder about the size of a juice cup. He withdrew a piece of folded metal from it that he levered open like a pocketknife, then screwed to a canister of gas. It was the smallest camping stove she had ever seen. He then pulled an array of bags and sachets from his pack and, in a single pot, created the most miraculous stew she had ever tasted. It was impossible to believe that it had been a collection of freeze-dried ingredients just minutes before.

Two enormous ravens took possession of a nearby tree, watching them eat and occasionally calling out to them with a deep, "Craw!"

"Smart birds," Hoodoo said. "They've figure out that humans mean easy food. They're omnivores, they'll sit and wait for any little tidbits we might leave behind."

"Huginn, and Muninn," Mallory replied.

"I'm sorry?"

"Norse mythology. Two ravens that represented pieces of Odin's mind, specifically his thoughts and memories. He would send them out into the world to watch the affairs of humans and report back to him," Mallory told him.

"You like mythology?" he asked.

"I do. Myths are our history, as sure as anything in the history books, if you can learn what they really mean. I'm named for a myth."

"Mallory? I don't remember that one," he said.

"No, my middle name. Cassandra. She was a Greek princess and prophet, but she was cursed by Apollo--" she fell silent for a long moment, realizing what she was about to say, "she was cursed that her prophecies would always be right, but that no one she told would believe her."

"Sounds awful. To know that you are right but to not be able to do anything about it."

"Yeah," Mallory said flatly.

They ate in silence after that and by the time they had finished eating, the sky was beginning to darken and the horizon was a dusky orange. "This is our home for tonight," Hoodoo said. "It's the best camp on this side of the mesa anyway, nice and flat, with a good view of the sky."

They couldn't see the actual sun from where they were, but they saw the orange and red light that it threw across the sky, and they watched that fade to black. The sky blazed with more

70

stars than she had seen in years. So far from any town or city, the light pollution was basically zero, so even the more subtle night sky components, like the Milky Way, were easily visible.

They talked about the granary, and Tevbaugh. Hoodoo told her the story of meeting his wife. They traded geocaching stories, but the weight of the things that neither was saying eventually slowed the conversation down as they danced around the topics.

"Can I... can I ask a kind of personal question?" Hoodoo said quietly.

Mallory looked a bit puzzled, but said, "Sure."

"Why did you agree to come out here?"

"What do you mean?" she asked, trying to sound as light and bright as she could.

"I wasn't sure that you'd agree to come with me. I know I kind of... made a joke out of it, gathering stuff up without asking you, but I was more than 80% sure that you were going to say no."

"Oh. Well..." her voice trailed off and she glanced up at the brilliant splash of stars that made up the Milky Way. Her hand absently went to the phone in her pocket and the photos that it contained. They were the only chance she'd ever have to prove that Toller was doing bad science, to make a name for himself. "I just need a break from the real world right about now."

"You aren't running from the law are you?" Hoodoo laughed.

"No. Not the law. My parents. My professors. I kind of... I kind of blew it."

They both stared into the sky for a long minute. The stars winked and glittered. Except for a small breeze pushing a leaf across the sand, there was no noise. Mallory felt like the world had come to halt.

"Exactly how much trouble are you in?" he asked in a low, serious voice.

"Well..." she sighed, and told him the story.

* * *

The morning after Mallory and Joyce pieced together what Toller was doing, that he was hiding any evidence that contradicted his theory about the site, possibly even destroying it, she had called in sick. She had called in the next day as well. She had picked up her phone a hundred times, contemplating which professor she could call to get advice, even dialing once and hanging up as soon as she heard a voice on the other end. Her father's words kept coming to her mind, the repeated refrain that had been her North Star since she was twelve: "Start with one right thing."

But she couldn't see it. There were so many paths, she just didn't know which one to start down. Publicly confront one of the most important people in her industry? Meekly accept what he was doing and continue her internship? Approach someone lower in the hierarchy? Call someone on the outisde? She wasn't even sure who she'd call with a problem like this. It wasn't like Toller had a boss. He *was* the boss.

Her stomach churned, and she felt on the verge of vomiting.

Pacing in her tiny room she had a thought: What would her mother do? How would Debbie Alday-Campbell approach this problem? She'd never been one for her husband's planned methodical approach to problems. She was much more... confrontational. Mallory could picture the scene in its entirety. Her mother would have walked into the site and laid down the law in that molasses thick southern accent of hers that made everything sound sweet, no matter how scathing the actual content. Mallory had seen her dress down everyone from policemen to preachers and usually walked away with *them* apologizing to *her*. If her father's approach wasn't working, would her mother's? It was the only path she could see.

She steeled herself and returned to work, determined to ask Toller about the sherd, hopefully in the most public way possible.

It didn't take very long for an opportunity to present itself. Toller crossed her path after just an hour on the site. It had to be now. If she waited any longer, she would never have the courage to try again. She pulled in a breath and stepped into his path. "Where is the sherd I found?" She tried to sound as conversational as possible, keeping the edge of adrenaline that she was feeling out her voice.

"I'm sorry, Miss... Campbell, was it?" he was pumping the charm, "I have a very important meeting near the kiva and I can't speak to you right now. Find me later." He turned and resumed his path toward the center of the site. Her stomach flipped again.

"Where is my sherd?" she called after him, her voice a bit louder. He continued away from her, undeterred. She pulled in a lung-full of air and pushed her voice to its edge. "WHERE IS MY SHERD?"

He stopped. The entire camp stopped and turned toward her. A few people in the periphery of her vision even stepped out of tents and trailers to see what was happening.

Toller stepped quickly back toward her, a look on his face that she was sure had silenced many an undergrad in its day. He quickly recovered his mask of calm and asked, "What on Earth has you so upset?" his voice fairly oozed with honey, "Come. Walk with me, let's talk about this." He reached up and placed a firm hand on her shoulder. She shook it off.

"No," she said, trying to sound as assured as she could, her volume pitched quite bit louder than his. "Let's talk here. Where is my sherd?"

"Your sherd? Yours?" he snorted, and turned to the troop of undergraduate lackeys who followed him everywhere. "Miss Campbell seems to believe that an archaeological find belongs to her rather than to humanity." They giggled uncomfortably, eyeing Mallory. "Excuse us Miss Campbell," he said, and he turned away from her again. Anger welled up in her.

"Where did you hide it? Where did you hide the proof that you're wrong? What else have you hidden? Who else here has found things that will never see the light of day because you're afraid of evidence that contradicts you?" Her voice was a shriek of tears and the words were a tumble. Around her she could hear the whispers and hisses of voices as a crowd of onlookers gathered.

In a firm, clear voice that cut across the chatter Toller said, "You're fired Miss Campbell. I don't know what in the world you're talking about, but I won't have you disrupting my site. Mitch," he said, motioning to one of the site supervisors, "please see that she's escorted off the reservation." He turned and walked away.

Mallory yelled after him, a tumble of incoherent accusations and words punctuated by bouts of crying and throat tearing screams as Mitch struggled to contain her and move her towards the entrance of the site. Her arms and legs flailed at the young man who seemed unable to elicit any help. Around her she could only see flashes of faces covered in shock. A group of young male workers laughed and pointed. An older woman shook her head, her face a map of disappointment and disgust. A man she had never seen before yelled from the side, dressing her down for disrespect. A group of girls covered their mouths and whispered to each other in gossipy tones.

For his part, Toller continued his slow walk away from her, stopping only once to look back at her, a smug smile on his face. After catching her eye, he shook his head and winked at her then went about his business, Mallory seemingly forgotten. She finally fell into silence and stopped fighting, her throat raw from screaming. She felt Mitch's firm hand on her elbow and turned to follow him, cowed.

* * *

"I must have looked like a lunatic," she told Hoodoo. "I can't imagine the rumors and stories that people are telling about me." She tucked a loose strand of hair behind her ear and wiped at a small tear.

"Do you think this guy, Toller, do you think he'll call your professors?" Hoodoo asked, a shocked look on his face.

"I don't know," she shrugged. "He probably already has."

"Do you... do you want to go back? To go home? You need to deal with this."

"No!" She nearly leapt at him. "No. I need a few days, Hoodoo, seriously. There's nothing I can do right now to fix this, and I need... I just need time."

He nodded his understanding and turned his face out toward the formation where they had spent the afternoon. "You did good out there today," he said. "You're a brave young woman. You'll figure out what to do."

"Thanks," she murmured.

"All right," he said, the sense of joviality back in his voice. "Then get some sleep. Big day tomorrow." He stood and dusted off his pants. "Hey," he called back as he walked away. She turned to look back at him. "Jonathan Toller's an idiot," he said. "Good night."

Sitting with her knees pulled up to her chest Mallory chuckled quietly to herself. She let the surge of adrenaline that had come with repeating the story drain away, watching the lights of planes cross the star-crowded sky. Soon, with just the light of a small LED lantern, Mallory brushed her teeth and unrolled a sleeping pad. The night was warm and close, and she didn't think she would need her sleeping bag, but she unrolled it to lie on top of it. From there, she watched Hoodoo's tiny light bob around towards the back of the stage, a respectful distance from her. She couldn't make out exactly what he was doing, though she thought she could see him turning pages in his notebook, silhouetted by his own lantern.

She pulled the small orange device that Lynn had given her out of her pack and depressed the "on" switch. When the small LED at the top indicated that the unit was ready, she pressed the "check in" button as Lynn had directed and waited for the LED to change to green. When it had, she turned the unit off and replaced it in her pack.

Turning her face towards the sky, she lay back letting her mind wander. Somewhere out there, Dr. Toller was probably laughing with his crew over a beer as she had seen him do so many times before. She knew that he felt secure in the knowledge that she was gone and that he'd never see her again. On the east coast, her family was probably getting ready for bed. She hoped that her mother wasn't too worried about her. Fixing this situation with Toller, and with her position at the university, had to be something she did herself. Perhaps spending three days in the desert looking for a mythic treasure wasn't the obvious way to do that, but it was a decision that she alone had control over and, for the minute, that felt great.

She settled into her sleep roll and scanned for any constellations that she could identify. She was asleep before she found one.

* * *

The next morning, in downtown Memphis, Utah, Lynn Estes arrived at Hoodoo Hiking Outfitters and parked her car behind the shop. There was a small car with North Carolina plates already parked there, and Lynn noticed with surprise that the passenger side window was rolled down. Had Mallory left it that way? Approaching the car, she realized that the window was not open: it had been smashed. The passenger seat was full of glass, and there were also a few pieces on the asphalt. Aside from a water bottle in the center console, the car was otherwise immaculately clean. There didn't appear to be anything in it. Whether that was because Mallory had stored everything in the trunk or because everything had been stolen, was unclear.

Lynn called Carey's cell but it immediately went to voicemail, as expected. They were they were outside cell coverage. She left a short voicemail then disconnected and called the sheriff. She described the situation to the deputy who answered, saying simply that someone had hired Hoodoo as a guide, and left her car at the store where it had been broken into, or maybe just vandalized. When asked, she had to admit that she didn't know when it had happened. She hadn't gone behind the store when she'd left the night before. They said they'd be by the store shortly and gave her permission to cover the exposed window with plastic, not that it was likely to rain that day.

Lynn chewed at her lip a bit, her habit when thinking, but couldn't see anything else that she could do about this at the moment. There wasn't a lot of crime in Memphis, but teenagers were easily bored out here in the wilderness and sometimes got into mischief.

She went toward the front of the store, intending to find plastic sheeting and to wait for the police. Instead, she found the door of the store standing open, glass and splintered wood littering the front stoop of the store. Inside, she could see that the store was in a higher degree of disarray than even usual. She slid past the window of the store and raised her cell phone to call the sheriff again. She needed someone there, and she needed them now.

* * *

Out on the mesa, Mallory woke up and looked around. There was a chill in the air, and she pulled a fleece cap from her bag and snugged it over her ears. She wasn't certain where Hoodoo had slept the night before, but she didn't see a sleeping pad rolled out anywhere. A few feet from her, towards the center of the clearing, the little camp stove sat with a pot on top, full of water. Beside it, she found two mugs, a packet of instant coffee, and a packet that was labeled "breakfast skillet." Inside the packet, she found freeze-dried eggs, potatoes and sausages. She lit the little stove and waited for the water to boil then mixed some with the coffee in one mug, and with the freeze-dried eggs in the other. She enjoyed the coffee while waiting for the eggs to rehydrate.

The two ravens returned, alighting again on the pine bough they had occupied before, and intently watched her every move.

"Morning Huginn," she said, nodding at them. "Muninn. Am I really the most interesting thing happening on Midgard right now? I can't believe Odin needs to know this much about me."

"Crawk! Crawk!" one of the birds called in reply.

She laughed a silent laugh and went back to her breakfast. Just as she finished up the eggs, which weren't bad but weren't exactly good either, Hoodoo strolled into camp from the narrow opening at the back. He was already dusty from the trail, with a twig lodged in his curls.

"You found your breakfast, I see!" he called as he approached her.

"Yeah, thanks." She said. "It was good."

"Those dehydrated things always taste like salty mush to me," he retorted, his lips quirking into distaste. He absently pulled the broken twig from his hair and tossed it aside. "I got up a few hours ago, as soon as there was a little light. I've been scouting. I think I've found a way over to the granary." He stepped in close and dropped his voice. "Are you sure you don't want to go back to town and call home?"

"I'm sure," she said with a curt nod that she hoped told him that she didn't want to discuss the problem any further.

"Okay. Then let's get on the trail... it's an interesting one. I'm not sure you're going to like it." He sounded like a child with a secret, his eyes dancing.

"Oh no. Better or worse than getting around that tree out on the ridge?" she asked, her stomach suddenly at her feet.

"Uh... depends on your point of view. You have to cross a pretty deep ravine. It isn't as high as the ridge, but it's pretty high. The good news is that there's a log across it. A nice sturdy ponderosa pine," he said.

"Have you been all the way to the granary? What did you find? Was there anything there?" The questions tumbled out of her in a rush. She wasn't sure when she had become so invested in this search, but it was clear to her that she had.

He laughed. "No, no. I waited for you to take the last leg. I just figured out how to get over there," he reassured her. "We'll go over together. It's really just four fins over that way, but we have to go around a few obstacles to get there." He waved his hand in the general direction of the granary.

Without much more ceremony, they packed up and started hiking. The first leg was a reverse of part of the previous day's hike, through the narrow opening at the back of the "stage," then down the side of the fin. A dozen turns later, and they arrived at a stone that they had climbed down yesterday from the top of a neighboring fin. It was a large boulder that was wedged between the two fins, as if it had fallen from some height.

She had expected him to climb the boulder, but instead he removed his pack and squatted down in front of the stone. He shoved his pack into an empty space below the boulder, and it disappeared. He lay on his back and stuck his arms into the hole after the pack. "Now it gets fun," he said. He raised his knees and pushed with his feet until his torso was completely under the rock then, in one swift motion, his legs disappeared into the hole as well. Mallory got onto her knees and peered through the opening. From the other side, he motioned and said, "Send the pack through first."

Mallory pushed the pack through, then mirrored his movements, pushing herself through with her feet, then pulling with her arms. He took her hands and assisted her on the last bit, getting her legs through. On the other side, they were in a small, enclosed area about the size of a large closet. There was a small crevice to one side that was less than a foot wide; towards the top of the wall, up about five feet, it opened to a wider V.

"We need to go up there," Hoodoo said, pointing up at the V. "I want you to go first this time, just get to the top and wait."

"Okay," she said. "Is it dangerous up there?"

"No," he said. "I can just help you better from behind." He knelt and formed his hands into a stirrup, which she stepped into, at the same time grabbing the top of the crevice with both hands and hauling herself up. She easily cleared the crevice and landed on top of the two pieces of stone. She found herself at the beginning of something that looked like a slot canyon with close walls that curved in sinuous shapes. The wide V of the crevice quickly rose into high walls, but there was no floor at the bottom, just a continuation of the crack.

She adjusted and tried to stand. Behind her, Hoodoo hoisted himself up with his arms then swung his legs over the edge, "Wait!" he said, "You have to crab walk, like this."

He jumped past her and quickly positioned himself so that his back was against the wall. His legs were straight out pressing against the opposite wall. He shifted a foot and slid his body to the side to follow it. "If you try to walk upright, you're going to break an ankle," he said.

She mimicked his body position and tried it for herself. Because she was shorter than him, she was further down in the V, but she found moving this way fairly easy. He quickly scuttled sideways and disappeared into the higher walls around the curve of the crevice. She moved into the crevice after him, trying to match his movements and positions.

The crevice wasn't long, but by the time they emerged on the other side, her hamstrings and calves burned with the effort. They had come out onto an open landing at the top of a fin. It was wide and flat, and she took the opportunity to sit and stretch her legs, trying to work out the tension that was now in them. Hoodoo paced near her doing stretches of his own.

He sat down beside her. "We're about halfway there. It might not seem like it, but we actually lost a little ground. We're about six fins over from the one we're targeting now. The good news is that it's mostly an easy walk."

"An easy walk sounds good," she said, "especially knowing that log you mentioned comes at the end of it."

80

"Then let's do it," he said, and shouldered his pack.

Hoodoo had been honest about the walk. They zigzagged a bit to avoid the deeper ravines and crevices between the fins, eventually arriving at a fin that was separated from the one that they were on by about four feet. Four feet had never looked quite as distant to Mallory.

Hoodoo scooted toward the edge and threw out one leg so that he was spread-eagle over the ravine. He reached both hands out to Mallory and said, "C'mon! Jump!"

She took his hands and took a few steps back, ran forward, then leapt, and Hoodoo used her momentum to swing her over the ravine and pull himself the rest of the way across.

"That was great! I'll make a canyoneer out of you yet!" Hoodoo laughed.

He crossed the fin and sat down on his heels at the edge, motioning for her to join him. She settled beside him, and they looked across an even wider ravine. On the other side, to her left and below them, was the crevice that held the granary. She couldn't see it from this angle, but she recognized the outline. To her right, just below the edge of the fin, was a large pine log that had long ago been stripped bare by wind and weather. The roots rested at the extreme edge of the crevice that held the granary, and from there it tapered up toward them, ending at a point a few feet below the edge of the fin they were on. She guessed that the log was wedged at an angle of about thirty degrees. The stumps of former branches stuck out of the log in random spots. Some had jagged remains of branches poking out, but others were little more than large bumps on the trunk.

"It looks like a ladder," Mallory said, her eyes moving back and forth across the log.

"It basically is, until about halfway down, then you run out of branch stumps and it's just a log," Hoodoo replied.

She scanned down the ravine. Both sides were sheer stone faces with very little differentiation in the surface. There appeared to be no handholds, or even cracks on the faces. Shadow and darkness filled the space between the walls before she could see the bottom. As far as she could see, the drop would be all the way to the desert below: several hundred feet.

"I don't know if I can do that," Mallory whispered.

"I'll admit, it's a little scary, even for me," he admitted. "I'll make it as safe as I can," he said.

He started pulling ropes and other equipment from his pack. There was a tangle of carabineers, and a cluster of thin straps that had been sewn into loops that he called a "sling." He pulled out two climbing harnesses and tossed one to her.

"Put this on," he said. While she stepped into it, he went over to a large boulder and laid his hand on top then kicked the bottom several times. He muttered, "No vibration." To her surprise he reared back and mule kicked the stone, which didn't budge. He then pulled one of the slings from the pile and looped it around the base of the large stone, fastening two carabineers to either end of the loop. He clipped a second sling into the carabineers, then pulled it down to a point where he tied a knot and placed another carabineer. He fed a line of rope through the carabineer and pulled it until he was roughly at the center of the length of rope. He tossed the rest towards the edge of the fin, just above the log.

"I'll anchor you to this when the time comes," he said, and helped her adjust the fit of the harness. He clipped a short piece of webbing with a carabineer at either end to the loop on the front of her harness. He put on his own harness and repacked his pack, leaving a long sling free. "I'll go over first, then we'll get you over."

He picked up the length of rope and walked backwards off the edge. She rushed forward and watched as he half walked, half slid down the short distance to the log. He then pulled the sling free, clipped it to the front of his harness, and tossed the other end underneath the log so that it came up on the other side. He clipped that end to his harness as well, effectively connecting himself to the log. He lowered his upper body so that he was using the log as a ladder and took a step or two backward, down the log, and then adjusted the position of the

82

sling, all the while pulling the rope along with him. He repeated the process until he reached the area of the log that had no branches. There, he gingerly lowered himself onto the log so that he was straddling it and scooted backwards, occasionally stopping to adjust the sling. At the root ball of the tree, he had to unclip himself and contort his body to pull himself partially over the roots and partially through. The whole process took about twenty minutes.

Soon he stood upright on the ledge and waved at her from behind the roots of the log. She watched as he removed slings and carabineers from his pack, constructing an anchor on his side of the ravine similar to the first. Then he fed the ends of the rope through and tied a series of knots. What resulted was a long loop of rope anchored to stone at either end. It roughly paralleled the log.

Hoodoo raised his hands to his mouth and called across the ravine, "Clip the carabineer that I put on your harness to that! Then just do what I did!"

"Okay!" she called back, trying to sound more assured than she was feeling. She attached the clip to the ropes and started reaching behind herself, using her toes to feel for the log. Unlike Hoodoo who had calmly walked backwards, Mallory was essentially laying on her face, searching for a foothold. "Just do what he did," she muttered to herself. She wished she had watched him more closely.

"A little left!" she heard Hoodoo yell behind her. She shuffled to the left and felt her foot connect. Reassured, she lowered herself the rest of the way and was soon ready to move down the "ladder" just as Hoodoo had done. She took several steps, carefully reaching behind to find the next. She studiously avoided looking to either side of herself, trying not to be aware of the drop she was dangling over. "Don't worry," Hoodoo yelled, "you could practically zipline down that rope! If you fall the rope will catch you."

Just as he said that, the branch beneath her left foot snapped and broke away! Mallory felt her weight shift in that direction, and she locked her right leg and her arms in attempt to keep herself from going over. She also felt the harness tug at her waist as the rope took some of her weight.

"You're okay!" Hoodoo yelled behind her. "Take a second to recover and keep coming!"

She blew out a long breath, cursing him a bit in her mind, and then continued. When she ran out of branches, she sat down on the log, just as he had. She kept her eyes intently on the log, desperately ignoring the fact that he feet were dangling in open air. Her stomach felt like a trout that had been tossed onshore. She pushed back and scooted the rest of the way, one arm length at a time. It felt like a year passed before the roots touched her back. She felt his hands on her shoulders, and Hoodoo helped her over the last obstacle, pulling her through the root ball. With her feet firmly on the stone, she let out a huge celebratory whoop and wrapped her arms around the thin Hoodoo in a bear hug. "I did it! I did it!" she laughed raucously, the sound echoing down the side of the mesa. "I deserve a reward," she whooped again. "Show me that granary!"

CHAPTER EIGHT

Sheriff's Deputy Alejandro Reyes stood in the middle of Hoodoo Hiking Outfitters and scanned the chaos. He knew that the shop looked like an in-progress yard sale on even the best of days but, with the door kicked in and the shelves looted, it currently looked like a hoarder's bedroom.

"Tell me this story again," he said and inserted his thumbs into his gun belt causing his chest to expand and his elbows to splay out to the side. He was already an imposingly large man, and the posture made him look even larger.

Lynn sighed, "Alex. This is a small town. I remember when you were 110 pounds soaking wet and you tried to keep your acne hidden by growing your hair out and wearing it in your face like some kind of... emo reject. Puffing your chest up isn't intimidating to me."

He relaxed a little and half-heartedly shrugged. "Sorry. Habit."

"Fine." She flicked a hand at him dismissively. "Please... I've been through this twice already. Believe me when I tell you this: I don't know who she was. I don't know where she found the map. I don't know who broke into the store. I don't know if it's related. But most of all, I don't know where she and Carey are now! I don't know. I don't know! I. Don't. KNOW!" She shook her hands in a gesture of exasperation.

The deputy's radio burped, and he held up a finger indicating that she should wait. A dispatcher reported, "Car comes back as registered to Mallory Ann Campbell, Pineville, NC. I called the associated phone number but it dumped to voicemail."

Reyes thanked her and turned his attention back to Lynn. "That was the name she gave you?"

"Yeah."

"It doesn't bother you that Hoodoo's out there in the wilderness, alone, with a nubile young co-ed?" Reyes said eyebrow arched.

"You're disgusting," she said, her face screwed into a look of distaste. "Nubile? Really?"

"It's a legitimate question," he retorted.

"Carey's been in the back country with everything from bachelorette parties to sororities, and I've never once even suspected a problem. Last March, he took that underwear catalog shoot out to Tirzah falls. If I can trust him with a literal pack of lingerie models, I can trust him with anyone."

"It had to be asked," he shrugged. "You say nothing was stolen from the store?" Reyes asked.

Lynn looked around. "The cash drawer was empty when I left last night, and the safe is still locked. They couldn't have taken any money. Otherwise..." she spread her hands and pointed all around herself, "it's hard to say for sure, but I don't think so..."

"You think they were looking for this Campbell girl?"

"I think... they were looking for the map," she said.

"Well... we've both seen people do crazy things when they thought they had a new lead on the Frenchman. You think they knew Hoodoo was taking her out to the mesa?" Reyes asked.

"I... don't see how, unless they got some information from her. I certainly haven't told anyone. As far as I know they were the only two people in the world that knew they were headed out there."

"You said she checked in with you last night?"

Lynn nodded wearily and shook her hand in a 'so-so' gesture. "Just a set of coords. The device I gave her is pretty rudimentary. I know where they were and that they were fine around 7:30 last night, but... that's it, really. I think I need to go find them."

He scrubbed at his closely cropped black hair with his palm, like he was trying to jumpstart his brain. "Yep. I reckon we do. Let's lock this place up as best we can, and get that car secured. We'll have to tow it I guess. Then we can head out toward the mesa. Daylight's burning."

The granary was a roughly cylindrical structure with walls made of rough stone mortared together with clay. It filled the space in a natural way, like a wasp's nest or a beehive, edges conforming to the shape of the crevice that held it. Mallory ran her fingers over the surface of the clay marveling at the construction. Towards the top, she found a mound of clay that had been forced into a separation between stones. The fingerprints of the builder were clearly visible in the clay. Were these the tips of Tevbaugh's fingers? Or those of a Native American from long ago? The Fremont Peoples inhabited these hills and canyons for over a thousand years, starting around 1 CE. The Anaszi had been in the area for a century or more before that. There was simply no easy way to know who had built the structure or when.

Towards the back of the structure, she found a large flat area that appeared to be entirely clay with no stones imbedded. It was rectangular and reminded her of the access panel in the back of a closet or a bathroom. The surface of it was smooth and unblemished. At the top of the granary, there was a similar area, except round, and framed with dry wood. There were no openings on the surface of the granary or any way to see inside. The top of the granary had separated from the roof of the crevice leaving a gap of about a half an inch. It was the only access point that she could see.

Hoodoo squatted beside the granary and stared at it. "What do you think?" he said.

"I... don't know. Half of me wants to just pull it down and see what's inside, but the other part of me is screaming that this is a potentially 2000 year old archaeological find and that I'm going to get myself kicked out of grad school."

"You're close enough to that already," he said.

"Exactly." She sighed and pulled off her backpack. In the top pocket was a headlamp. She clicked it on and tried to position it so that it shone into the gap at the top of the granary, then strained to see inside. She could see the light play across the stone ceiling, but little else. She pulled out her smartphone and swiped through screens until the camera was active and held that up to the crack. She could see only blackness on the screen, even with the flash on.

Hoodoo stood at the edge of the crevice pushing his thumbs into the small of his back and rocking on the balls of his feet in a gesture of thinking. He had shucked his harness, and it was lying in a heap to one side of the ledge with all of the climbing equipment that he had pulled from his pack. He picked up her harness where she had dropped it and tossed it into the pile, then turned, a thoughtful look on his face, and opened his mouth as if he were about to speak. Before he produced a sound, he was hit by a spray of rock and dirt as a portion of the ceiling exploded into fragments. The sound of the gunshot echoed into the crevice a fraction of a second later.

"Down!" Hoodoo screamed, and shoved Mallory toward the back of the small crevice that held the granary. She had no time to register what was happening. A second spray of stone and dirt fell from the wall of the crevice, followed quickly by the report of the second shot.

"Is that a gun?" she screamed incredulously.

"Don't know what else it would be," he retorted.

"Who is it?'

"Dunno, but whoever it is out there is shooting wild," he said.

"Why is someone shooting at us?!" Mallory nearly screamed.

"Dunno. People get territorial about this mesa. A lot of folk think that treasure already belongs to them." He craned his neck, trying to see over the ledge without moving his body into a line of fire. "Nobody ever shot at me before, though," he growled.

She pulled back, deeper into the crevice. "Where are they?"

"They could be above us or below us. Maybe that's why the shots are so wild; they can't find the angle to compensate for the height difference." Hoodoo slid forward and hooked his toe into the strap on his pack pulling it towards them as the sound of a third shot reached them, even though they didn't see evidence of a bullet strike this time.

"The lights!" Mallory breathed.

"What?"

"The lights I saw down on the ground. That could have been reflections off a binocular lens," she said.

"Or a rifle scope. Did you tell anyone we were coming out here?" Hoodoo asked.

"Just my brother... he's in North Carolina!"

"Did anyone overhear you?" he demanded.

"I don't… I don't think so. I was in the alley behind the store when I called him, but I didn't even really say where we were going. What does it matter? Did you tell anyone? Maybe Lynn told someone!"

"I doubt that," Hoodoo responded. "It doesn't matter, I guess. We just have to figure out how to get out of here. We're sitting ducks. As soon as this idiot figures out his shooting angles…"

Mallory rose up on her knees and looked back towards the log they had climbed in on. "We can't go back that way. We'll be even more exposed!" Another bullet smacked into the front of the granary sending a spray of dried mud and rock into the air. Mallory fell back, instinctively trying to hide herself as best she could. She felt her elbow connect with the granary wall, and she heard a crack that sounded like a terra cotta pot splintering.

Looking behind her, she realized that she had accidentally fallen into the large flat area of clay on the wall, cracking it. An area in the center had fallen away. She leaned forward, pushing the other shards with the heel of her hand until she had opened a gap wide enough to fit through. "Forgive me," she whispered to the long dead person who had constructed the granary, be it Tevbaugh, or someone else.

She realized that she was still holding the smartphone in her hand, and the flashlight was still activated. She shoved her hand inside, and the interior of the granary bloomed into light. It was an empty space.

She clambered inside, leaving Hoodoo tentatively straining to see over the edge of the crevice trying to spot the shooter. The interior was much like the exterior with the addition of some spider webs. On the outside of the structure, the crevice had come to a sharp corner, but here, on the inside, there was a gentler slope. Painted on the wall was a blocky, triangular figure with a circle behind its head. Mallory instantly recognized it as the first of the three female figures that had been drawn on the map.

She pressed the camera button on the phone and snapped a photo of the figure then shone the light of the flash over the surface. It was another clay wall, like the one she had just broken through! She kicked at it, and it shattered, falling away in large pieces. Behind it was a low horizontal opening that looked like a mail slot in a door.

There was a faint dusky light coming from somewhere beyond her vision.

"Hey!" she yelled at Hoodoo, sticking her head out of the granary, "In here!" She ducked back inside and began crawling through the opening that she had found. She could hear Hoodoo behind her, pulling his much larger frame into the granary with grunts and exhalations.

She found herself in a long, low tunnel. It wasn't quite tall enough for her to come completely onto her hands and knees. Instead, she was on her stomach pulling herself forward with her hands, and pushing with her toes as best she could manage, shoving her pack ahead of her. Ahead she could see a bright light.

She soon emerged into a large opening. She quickly scanned the area seeing that it was a roughly cylindrical, cave-like room open to the sky above. It was like being at the bottom of a large well. The walls towered above her for several stories leaving only a small circle of sky visible above. To one side was a thin opening, like a slot canyon that was not wide enough for a human to fit through. On the opposing side was another opening that extended for a few feet into the rock before closing up. The walls were pockmarked with small holes that had eroded in the wind. The center of the area was dominated by a large, brilliantly white hoodoo.

She ran back to the opening where she had emerged and stuck her head in. "It's a dead end!" she called back to Hoodoo who was about half way through the tunnel.

"What does it look like?" he grunted.

She described the room in broad strokes as he pulled himself through the last few feet. She helped him by pulling his pack through. He stood, looking around the room, taking in their situation.

"I thought I'd seen every square inch of this mesa by now. I had no idea this was here. How have I not found this before?" Suddenly he smacked his forehead with the heel of his hand. "Half my climbing gear is back out there on the granary ledge."

"All of it?" She asked and peered up the length of the walls.

"I grabbed my pack... there's some stuff in it, but it isn't much." He dug his fingers into his thick beard, tugging at the strands. "We can't risk going back out there in daylight. Whoever is shooting will figure out the angles soon enough."

He went to the wall and reached up to one of the holes, testing it for his weight, then looked back at her, chewing at his lip. "I suppose the good news is that if they try to follow us they'll have to find their way through that maze of fins to get over to the ledge. That wasn't easy."

"Wait... is there *bad* news?"

He tugged at his beard again. "All the climbing anchors and ropes are still in place... so they'll have a pretty easy time of it," he said.

"Who do you think it is?" she asked.

He shook his head. "Another treasure hunter? An overzealous landowner? Someone who thinks we're getting too close to... I don't know! I've never been shot at before." He peered up at the sky, "I think I could climb out, but without harnesses it would be hard to get you out too." He turned towards the low opening and swore a bit. "I think my belay equipment is still out there too."

"Wouldn't we be just as vulnerable up there as we were out on the ledge?" Mallory looked up to the sky as well, trying to get any hint as to what might be up there.

"I dunno. It depends on where the shooter actually is," he shrugged.

"Okay... Well, Tevbaugh got us into this, maybe he can get us out of it." She pulled her phone from her pocket and brought up the photo of the pictograph that she had found inside the granary. The photo was a bit blurry, and the figure was barely in the frame, thanks to the haste she took the photo with, but it was visible. "I saw this inside the granary." She explained the second wall that she had found inside and how she had kicked through it to find the opening.

Hoodoo walked a tight circle around the white formation in the center of the room. "So, this is his first goddess? What does he say?"

"He says that we'll need to 'pray to the mother,'" Mallory said, reading the words from the photo of the map on her phone.

"How do we pray to this?" he asked, with incredulity. "We don't have time for this. We need to find a way out of this box and off this mesa."

"Calm down!" Mallory said, placing a hand lightly onto his chest. "We followed his clues to get here. Our best chance to get out is to follow his clues. So what do we know?"

"That we have to pray," he sighed.

"We also know that this goddess is a mother. Who would Tevbaugh have prayed to?" she asked.

"I don't know. Could it be an Indian goddess? White Buffalo Woman?" he shrugged.

"First: Native American. And second: White Buffalo Woman is a plains myth. The native population here would have had very different myths…" She paused and looked up at the statue. "Wait. The Frenchman had a rosary in his things when he died. Could this be Mary?"

"As a very good lapsed Catholic I have to say, Mary isn't a goddess," he said, holding a hand up.

"Okay… no… but she's a mother. And Catholics do pray to her for… intercession, or whatever" she said, hopefully.

"No… we ask her to pray *for* us… Whatever," he conceded. "I don't want to debate theology right now. Let's just say this is Mary. What does that get us?"

"Well… I don't know. I'm Baptist," she said, and slumped onto the ground. "One right step," she muttered to herself.

"What?" Hoodoo asked.

"Nothing. It's something my dad taught me. 'One right step.' You can solve any problem if you think about each step first." She sighed. "I just have no idea what the problem here is, much less the steps."

She looked up at the white pillar-like formation in front of her. From the angle, it actually did look like a female form. She could make out a head and shoulders and, with a bit of imagination, she could see the traditional hand positions for a statue of Mary: left hand near her heart, right hand extended.

Mallory shifted her position moving onto her knees as if she were praying and looked up at the formation again. From this angle, she realized that the circular opening at the top of the walls formed a perfect halo behind the "head." She moved her eye down the length of the formation. Toward the base of the stone pillar was a smaller, thinner rock spire. From her position on her knees, she could see that the smaller rock protuberance pointed up towards one of the circular holes in the wall. She looked around herself. There were dozens of holes in the walls, so the fact that the rock pointed at one of them was probably a coincidence. On the far wall, she noticed that there were five holes that were in a straight line, vertically up the wall. She shifted position until the small spire pointed directly up at those five.

For the first time, she noticed that there was a white inclusion in the stone wall just below the five holes. It was a horizontal line, but when she aligned the spire of rock with the inclusion, it formed a cross.

She looked again at the holes in the walls. They went around the circumference of the room in a rough ellipse. She thought that if she could draw a line on the wall, starting with the hole at the top of the vertical row of five, the line would easily connect all of the holes around them and come back to the start like a string of beads.

"How many beads are on a rosary?" she quietly asked.

"Uhm..." Hoodoo started ticking off fingers, "Our Father, three Hail Marys, Hail Holy Queen, ten Hail Marys..." his voice faded as he counted. "Sixty," he finally responded. "Plus the cross at the end."

She marked an 'X' in the sand in front of her and stood up. "Count," she said, "double check me." She started counting the holes in the walls. Once he realized what she was doing, he started his own count. When she had finished, she waited patiently for him to conclude his count. "How many?" she asked, when he looked back at her.

"Sixty," he said, a twinkle in his eye.

"That's what I count too," she said and took his elbow. She pulled him to the position where she had been before, marked with the 'X,' then guided him onto his knees. He looked up and saw the cross formed by the spire of rock and the inclusion.

"I get it," he said.

"Okay then, mister 'good lapsed Catholic,' teach me how to pray a rosary," she said.

"You start with the crucifix, pray a prayer called the Apostle's Creed."

"Okay. We have the cross. Then what?" she replied.

"An 'Our Father,' then three 'Hail Marys,'" he counted four of the holes that formed a vertical line up from the cross, "and then..." he continued, but fell silent.

"Yes?" she prompted.

"Well... next is the first large bead..." he scratched at his temple. "There's a couple different ways to go here. You could say another 'Our Father,' or a 'Fatima,' or a 'Glory Be,' or… all of them, or some combination of them…" He looked at her and shrugged.

"I don't know if it's the prayers that are important or the number of beads," she said. "What comes next?"

"Well… then it's this thing called 'Announcing the Mystery.' The problem here is that there are a bunch of different mysteries. You could say the Sorrowful Mysteries, the Joyful Mysteries…"

"Okay, skip that for the moment, we can discuss that if it's the type of prayer that matters. What's next?" she waved her hand impatiently.

"They're called 'The Decades,' ten 'Hail Marys' then the next mystery. That repeats five times, until you get back to the big bead. You finish up with a prayer called 'Hail Holy Queen.'" He walked over to the wall where the five vertical holes were. The highest was about at his head level. He peered inside. "It starts and stops here. Maybe this is the key?"

He stuck his foot into one of the lower holes and lifted himself up so that he could see inside. The hole was irregularly shaped, seemingly cut by wind and water into the walls. This one was about the shape and size of a basketball.

"I don't see anything," he said, voice strained with the effort of supporting himself by one foot. He reached in with one hand and felt the sections of the hole that he could not see, his other hand gripping the edge of another hole nearby. "Wait," he said. His face pinched into an expression of someone straining to hear a faraway sound. He jumped down. "Let me see your phone." She handed it to him and he swiped the camera on, and then climbed back up. He extended the camera into the hole and maneuvered the screen a bit. "Ha!" he yelled, and jumped down again.

She took the camera from him and looked at the photo he had shot. Clearly in the middle of the screen she saw the letters 'AS' carved into the top of the hollow. She looked up to see him reach over to the second hole and feel the roof. "This one says… 'FR' I think." He reached for the third hole but couldn't quite reach it. He swung his body, each hand in a different hole, then brought his left and right hands together in a single hole, leaving his feet dangling. He rocked back and forth again and his left hand shot out as he moved to the third hole, like a child on monkey bars. "In here… 'OB," he said.

"One right step," Mallory said quietly smiling to herself. She smoothed the sand in front of her and began to transcribe what he called out. Some had pairs of letters others had three letters. Hoodoo swung from hole to hole, easily at first, the taut muscles of his arms supporting him but, as he neared the end, she could hear his grunts as he pulled himself high enough to feel the hidden letters. She could see the tremors in his forearms as he pushed himself. When he had finished the entire loop, he fell roughly to the ground and slumped into a seated position. Mallory pulled a bottle of water from her bag and took it to him, watching him greedily gulp about half of it.

"Tell me all that actually spelled something," he said.

She went back to the long list of letters that she had scratched into the sand. It read:

AS FR OB ING HU THO GH VA ED NO KI ABO VH BO
ALM VC WET HI CR TH WAS BN VES VU NG THE CV MO LO
OO DA BEG VI OBE DO GH XI ACE KO LOP FI HE NIN WLK
LOW YE REW VB NO HA JIM KLV CH BIP DSL

"It could be a cipher," she said, her face covered in doubt. "There are a few words in there: wet, the, beg, low... that doesn't help. Is there a prayer that will help?"

"I'm certainly about to start praying..." he snorted.

"Tell me about the mysteries," she said, pressing the fingers of both hands into her hair. "We skipped that part before."

"Uh... the rosary is really just a form of meditation," he said, between sips of water, "the mysteries are what you are supposed to be meditating on. There are different..." his voice trailed off as he noticed that she wasn't paying attention any more.

"The thing you meditate on..." she muttered as she dropped to her knees beside the grid of letters. "Ten Hail Marys then a Mystery right?"

"Kind of... you start with announcing a mystery, then say ten Hail Marys," he explained.

"Got it," she reached out and underlined the first letter pair, AS, then counted ten groupings and underlined the second, ABO. She continued until she had AS ABO VES OBE LOW. "As above, so below," she quoted.

The sound of another shot muffled by rock and distance echoed through the stone room.

"I don't think we can wait to figure this out." Hoodoo said, the exasperation plain in his voice. "We need to find our way out of here before they find their way to us. That shot was probably an attempt to see if we were still out on that ledge." He pulled himself up and paced to the thin crack in the high wall and peered inside, scanning up and down. He crossed the opening and walked the one or two steps that he could into the other side. "This opens up pretty wide once you get in there, and it slopes down. I think we could pass if we could get past this initial narrow point. He kicked at the ground angrily then stopped and kicked again. He looked back into the crack then knelt and started scooping loose sand away from the opening. "Bring me the trowel in the pocket on the left of my pack!" he called over his shoulder.

Mallory grabbed the trowel and ran to him. It was tight in the tiny crevice, but she could see over his shoulder. At the base of the crack, the opening widened a bit, and the more he dug, the wider it opened. He fell back, exhausted. She helped him to his feet and then knelt at the crack herself, taking up where he had left off.

"Get our packs together and eat something. I'll keep digging," she instructed. She heard him move away and the sound of fabric rustling and zippers being zipped. When he got back, she had moved a large quantity of sand, and the opening was much more visible. It would be tight, but they could probably slip through. "Not as much of a dead end as I thought," she said, standing.

"Let me go first," he said, and started shoving his pack through. It popped through the narrow opening like a wine cork and tumbled down the slope on the other side until it wedged between the walls. Hoodoo lay down and stuck his arms through, using his hands on the other side to find purchase and pull himself through. He grunted loudly as a stone dug into his hip, but adjusted, corkscrewing sideways. A few seconds passed where he didn't move at all. With a renewed effort, he leveraged his arms and pulled himself the rest of the way through kicking his feet a little.

Mallory dropped her pack and pushed it through, but a thought occurred to her and she ran back to the side of the white hoodoo that she now thought of as "Mary." She quickly snapped photos of the hoodoo and the letter grid, then kicked sand and dirt over the grid, and walked back and forth over it a few times, obliterating any hint of it.

Back at the narrow opening, she wriggled through assisted by Hoodoo, who pulled her lightly and kept her from tumbling down the ravine. On the other side of the opening, she was greeted with a narrow passage with a stony bottom. The square stones looked like an irregular staircase descending into twilit gloom.

Hoodoo pressed a power bar into her hand saying, "Keep your energy up. It might be a while before we can eat a real meal." He turned and started down the ravine keeping his hands on the walls on either side to maintain his balance.

They descended for a long thirty minutes; the walls beside them climbing ever taller. There was an occasional chockstone to climb over or a log to scoot under. It wasn't a steep descent, but it was steady and, as they went deeper, they donned headlamps to augment the weakening sunlight. It felt as if they were walking on the bottom of an ocean.

When the floor of the gigantic crack leveled out, they started noticing perpendicular cracks in the walls. Most were shallow and didn't appear to go anywhere. Hoodoo scouted a few that extended past their view, but he always came back saying that the crack had closed to an impassible width. They knew that they were travelling towards the center of the fin formation but little else.

Soon they came to a slightly wider area where a perpendicular crack crossed the one they were travelling in. They sat down on the sandy flat floor and ate another power bar. Mallory felt exhausted and couldn't imagine what Hoodoo was feeling.

"Low on water," Mallory said, taking a deep pull at the drinking tube that was extending from her pack.

"Yep. We aren't quite down to the level of the desert floor, but we might find some down here. Keep your eye out. There are a few springs around. After this snack, I'll explore these two side paths," he said, wearily.

She slumped against the wall and allowed her tiredness to unfocus her eyes. "Who do you suppose the cat goddess is?"

"Hmm?"

"If the next goddess wants us to 'See as the cat,' it must be a cat goddess, right?

"You're the mythology expert, not me," Hoodoo said, "I didn't even know there were cat goddesses."

"Oh, a couple," she answered. "Hecate, Greek goddess, could take the form of a black cat. The Norse didn't have any cat goddesses exactly, but Freya had a chariot that was pulled by cats. It could be Bast, I suppose," she said, trying to recall any other cat gods she had heard of.

"Bast?"

"Egyptian. Probably the most famous cat goddess. Any reason a French miner and gold hunter would know anything about an Egyptian goddess?"

"Tevbaugh wasn't technically French. He was Algerian."

"What? Why is he called 'The Frenchman' then?"

"He spoke French, and has a French sounding name. What would you call him?"

"Why was there an Algerian in Utah in the late 1800s?" Mallory asked incredulously.

Hoodoo released a deep breath, puffing out his lips. "Uhm… Lots of legends. No one knows. Lots of gold prospecting in the southwest. Lots of mining for every mineral you can name, really. Lots of mining in Africa too. He may have come here with some secret mining technique that he wanted to try out." He shrugged.

"Doesn't sound like that's the legend you believe though," she said.

"I think he came here from Egypt to teach the Mormons how to grow cotton. They came down here from Salt Lake after the Mormon War…"

"Mormon War?"

"Do they teach you nothing in college? When President Buchanan tried to… It's a long story. Anyway. Yes. The Mormon War. Brigham Young was the governor at the time. He wanted to ensure state independence, so he sent a bunch of settlers down here on the 'Cotton Mission,' to learn to grow cotton and tobacco and a couple other things that need a warm climate, all so that they didn't have to rely on imports. It's where the name of this area came from."

"Memphis? That's a city in Egypt too, y'know, not just Tennessee. "

"I meant 'Dixie.' The nick name for this area, and the name of the National Wilderness Area."

"Ah. Got it. Interesting," she said.

"I've heard he was a member of the French Foreign Legion…" he trailed off.

Mallory relaxed her shoulders, and her head lolled back against the warm stone. Her eyes unfocused, and she could feel the weariness of the day bearing down on her. Her eyes followed the line of the sandstone up to the sinuous line of the sky above them. She followed it away into the distance, then back across the ground to where Hoodoo sat with his eyes down and head forward resting on his knees. Suddenly something behind his head struck her. She sat up a little straighter and stared at the wall. An idea bubbled to the top of her mind. She pointed to the crack behind him, "No need to explore. We need to go down that one. That's where the path goes next."

CHAPTER NINE

Hoodoo craned his neck to see the point above his head that Mallory was indicating. He stood and found himself face-to-face with a carving in the stone wall about a quarter of an inch deep. It was distinctly man made, immaculately chiseled into the wall.

"A heart?" Hoodoo asked, incredulity sneaking into his voice.

"Yes! Don't you see?" Mallory whooped, nearly ecstatic. "As above, so below!"

"I don't get it," he admitted, fingers tracing the shape of the heart.

"The top part of the map... the part you showed me back in the shop... you said it traced out a route at the top of the fins, right?" She gesticulated upward, through the crack, at the sliver of sky high above them. "The first symbol on the map is a heart, and the trail starts at a heart-shaped rock fall?" She smacked the stone with a flat palm and repeated: "As above. So below! That path across the top is 'above,' this is the beginning of the trail 'below.'"

"You think the same pattern from the top will work down here?" He shifted and peered down the thin alley marked by the heart.

"I do! Yeah!" she gesticulated at the heart again as if this should be obvious to him.

He puffed out his lips and exhaled. "We don't really have a better option." He unzipped his pack and dug around, finally pulling out an ancient orange t-shirt, which he tossed at her. She shook it open and looked at the print on front: it was the first panel of the Frenchman's map, the one he had shown her back in the shop. She followed the line on the map from the heart to the next icon. The print on the shirt was chipped with age, be she could make out the deer.

"If I'm right, there should be a deer down there somewhere," she said as she started down the trail between the two high walls.

The stone walls here were unlike anything Mallory had ever seen. It was like walking down very narrow alleys between windowless buildings. The gigantic stone blocks on either side of her extended stories into the sky but, in most places, she could touch both walls with her outstretched arms. Above her head, the contours of the blocks softened and started to look like the lumpy hoodoo columns that were everywhere in the region. Every fifty or sixty feet, a perpendicular crack ran off in both directions, reinforcing the feeling that she was walking on gridded streets. At each intersection, she closely examined the walls looking for the petroglyph of the deer or something like it. It took seven intersections before she began to doubt herself. Was this right? Was she misinterpreting the map? She scraped at the wall with the heel of her hand trying to remove centuries of dust that might be obscuring the deer that she knew had to be under there, somewhere.

The enormity of what was happening suddenly crashed around her: they were in the middle of the desert, low on water, effectively lost, with a gunman somewhere behind them. She put her back to the wall and slid to a seated position resting her forehead on her knees. Her thoughts drifted through the last two days reconstructing their path here. She reached behind herself and unzipped a side pocket on her pack. The little orange emergency beacon Lynn had given her tumbled into her hand. Should she check in again?

She wished there was some way to send a message with the device. What would she even say?

She stared down the path at Hoodoo who was several intersections behind her still examining walls and scouting side paths. She'd just wait until he caught up to her so that they could decide their next move. She tilted her head back to look up at the darkening sky. It was late afternoon, and the amount of sunlight filtering into the deep cracks was steadily lessening.

With her head back, she saw it. A dark shape scratched into the rock face about fifteen feet down the right path. She scrambled up, her pack throwing her off balance, and ran down the path hastily shoving the emergency beacon back into its little pocket. There on the wall was the deer: large, almost life size, scratched into surface and then filled with charcoal. She had expected something smaller, comparable in size to the heart, which had been fist-sized. At an angle, this had looked like nothing more than a dark mineral patch in the stone.

She ran back to the intersection and whistled sharply. Hoodoo looked up at her and started loping in her direction.

A second sharp whistle echoed through the rocks, answering hers. Hoodoo stopped dead, a look of worry and bewilderment crossing his face. He slowly turned his head in the direction they had been traveling.

A third whistle floated ominously through the cracked stone. One long sharp note.

Hoodoo's eyes widened, and he started towards her at a quick gallop. He quickly closed the distance between them and skidded to a stop beside her nearly knocking her back to the ground.

"We need to move," he whispered harshly. "I don't know where they are or how many of them there are but we need to get ahead of them." He looked around at the options of directions they could travel.

"That way," Mallory said, breathlessly, "I just found it." They turned and jogged down the crack at a brisk pace.

"What's the next symbol?" Mallory asked, juggling the shirt and trying to orient it.

"Ladder!" he said quietly over his shoulder scanning the walls around them.

"There!" she said, indicating a path to the left with a shaky, child-like drawing of a ladder etched into the wall.

They continued down the path at a breakneck pace turning at the sigils of a house, a knife, a cactus, a feather... some were high, some low. With repetition, the images became easier to spot and soon they were running almost unimpeded by the need to search for symbols, taking the corners at a rapid pace and occasionally skidding on the loose gravel underfoot. They passed other signs: crossed arrows, a bear, a buffalo, a horse, signs that did not appear on the Frenchman's map, false signs to distract or lead them astray.

Soon, Mallory's pace slowed, her energy flagging. A day in the desert without a lot to eat or drink was taking its toll, and she was unused to running, especially with a pack.

"I can't!" she called, bracing herself against the wall. "I need..." she gasped, and sat down heavily.

Hoodoo sat on his heels beside her and quietly said, "Wait here. Rest. I still have a little in me. You can stop for a bit and I'll scout. You rest but keep an ear out."

Mallory nodded and slumped a little deeper. Hoodoo pulled off his pack and dropped it beside her. She listened to the chuff of his boots on the gravel and sand as he walked away from her. She closed her eyes resting her head on the rough stone behind her. She concentrated on slowing her ragged breathing.

She hadn't fallen asleep exactly, but she had felt her mind drifting downwards as it responded to the tiredness she felt. Suddenly she was alert. Something had changed in her surroundings; there was a sense of presence about her, something at the edge of perception. She turned her head, looking into every shadow, holding her breath. She strained her hearing, trying to catch anything around her.

"... boot..." she heard a tiny sound just at the edge of her perception, heard as if through a wall. Her head snapped in the direction she thought the sound had come from. She could see down the path in the dwindling light, but there was nothing there. She closed her eyes turning her head slightly, orienting an ear toward the sound. At first, she heard nothing but her own heartbeat pounding, loud as the ocean, then: "... stupid girl..." The sound was closer now and, if she strained, she could hear a general mumble of punctuated conversation though she couldn't make out words.

She scrambled to her feet and scooped up Hoodoo's pack, jogging down the same path he had taken. She quickly arrived at an intersection and scanned the ground for his tracks. Suddenly, she realized that this was exactly what the gunmen were doing. She looked back down her own path at the clear imprints of her boots... but what could she do about it? There was nothing here, no tools to rake the trail, or branches to brush behind her. She dropped both packs and ran, turning left, then right, and right again until she crossed her own path. If she couldn't hide her tracks, perhaps she could use them to her advantage.

She ran that way for several minutes, dodging in and out of the cracks in the stone, crisscrossing her own path until she ran into a partially blocked path. There was a stone here about fifteen feet high with rubble at the base and a squared off top. It appeared to be a fragment of the wall from high above that had given way and slid down to the desert floor. She examined it, identifying hand and foot holds. She could climb it.

She ran back to the point where she had dropped the packs, momentarily confusing even herself with the abundance of tracks she had left behind. At the packs, she paused and listened intently. She couldn't hear anything, and she hoped against hope that she wasn't making so much noise that they were able to hear her. With both packs she made her way back to the stone she had seen. She pulled a length of rope from Hoodoo's pack and looped it through the shoulder straps of both packs, looping the other end around her waist.

The climb was relatively easy, with clear steps and holds. If she had been rested and calm, she might even have enjoyed the challenge. As it was, the muscles in her arms vibrated with the effort, and her knees threatened collapse with each exertion. Only the terror of whoever was behind her propelled her to the top of the stone. On the top, she found a wide, flat ledge with about the area of a king-sized bed. If she could pull herself back to the edge where the stone met the wall of the canyon, she would be out of sight from below.

Using the last of her strength, she pulled the packs up and pushed everything to the back of the stone. She huddled in beside the packs, trying to make herself as small as she could manage. All she could do was listen and hope. She needed not only to listen for the men, but for Hoodoo. He'd have no idea where she was and may not know that they were no longer alone in the labyrinth of cracks and alleys.

Alone on the top of the rock, she finally felt her heart rate go down, though she could still feel every heartbeat thumping in her palms, held flat against the rock. She was no less scared, but the physical effects of her dash through the maze were lessening at least. She tried to slow her breathing and widen her senses, straining to hear each sound. There wasn't much. The desert here in this maze of cracked rocks was a sensory deprivation chamber. There was little wind and, in the gathering darkness, there were no birds or other wildlife active. She wondered where Hoodoo was. Had the people following them found him? Was he hiding somewhere else in the maze? Was he simply lost?

She actually saw them before she heard them. The sweep of a flashlight beam went up the wall in front of her then back down to the floor of the crack. She pulled in a breath, and her body went rigid. Below, she heard the crunch of gravel and sand as someone followed the arc of the light. To her right, a circle of light fell on the wall and stayed there, only scanning up and down. The glow of a second flashlight appeared to her

106

left, and she heard the sound of someone going deeper into the crevice.

"Anything?" a rough male voice said, then the sound of a lighter and a flare of light, followed by the sound of someone inhaling deeply through a cigarette. The footfalls continued to her left, softening as they receded. Silence fell over the canyon. Mallory could hear only the sound of her own breathing which she tried to time to the sound of the man smoking. She could smell the cigarette smoke. Suddenly the man's flashlight flipped to her side of the ravine filling the wall just above her head and slowly scanning downward. Mallory pulled into herself. She heard the man below take a few steps. Was he trying to see the top of the stone where she was hiding? She watched as the circle of light slid towards her shoulder. She pulled away from it, willing herself invisible.

A second light played on the wall to her left drawing her attention that way. Behind her, the probing circle of the first light dropped back down to the floor of the ravine, pointing down the path toward the man who had to be approaching from that direction. She listened as the crunch of boots grew louder. Mallory released a shuddering breath and blinked away a tear.

As the sound of the approaching man grew louder, she shifted in her hiding place hoping that the sound of the man walking would mask any noise that she was making. Soon, she was flat on her stomach. The stone radiated safety, which she absorbed into herself, gathering the courage she knew she would need.

"Tracks go back there for a bit," a new voice said. It was another man, but the voice was less rugged, and he sounded younger, "then they double back this way. Looks like it was just her, the feet are small."

The first man made a sound of disgust and muttered a few harsh sounding words under his breath. "C'mon. Too dark. We'll have to camp. Don't worry. We'll get 'em. They can't have gotten too far, and they can't move in the dark either."

Mallory listened to the sound of footfalls as they retreated and slowly pulled herself to the edge of her perch. Below her, silhouetted by their flashlights, were two men. One was tall but whip thin, wearing a rumpled cowboy hat and a flannel shirt with jeans. He carried a rifle in his left hand loosely holding it near the bolt. He looked like a rancher, or a cowboy. Beside him was a smaller man in a ball cap. He wore a short-sleeved shirt and loose cargo pants. The younger man carried a large pack, while the older was unburdened. They turned, and the glow of their flashlights receded into one of the side paths.

A short lifetime passed, but she saw nothing else. The men were gone, but there was no sign of Hoodoo either. She rolled onto her back and watched the last light of the day fade from the sky.

"Okay girl," she whispered. "Adventure time is over. If we're getting out of this alive, you have to get help." She pulled out her cell phone and pressed the home key, shielding the light of the screen in case anyone was looking. The screen flashed "NO SERVICE," which was what she had expected. Besides that, the battery indicator read "3%." She fished in the pocket of her pack and retrieved a small lipstick sized battery pack and plugged it into the phone. Immediately the battery indicator switched to "CHARGING."

Next on the agenda was food. She unzipped Hoodoo's pack and rummaged through it. His leather bound notebook fell out along with an assortment of loose climbing gear and other odds and ends. She finally reached the stratum that held the food. There were several packets of freeze dried foods: stroganoff, fried rice, chili mac, Hawaiian chicken. Her mouth watered at the sound of them, but she knew that there was barely any water left. She needed something that she wouldn't have to rehydrate. At the bottom of the stuff sack, she found a heavy freezer bag with dried blueberries, apricots and chunks of dried apple, which she dug into greedily.

When the empty pit in her belly began to feel sated, she took the last step available to her: she pulled out the small orange device that Lynn had given her. She pressed the ON/OFF button until an LED flashed at the top then settled into a steady red glow. She pressed the SOS button. The LED went through a cycle of flashing three times followed by a five second pause then three flashes. After five repetitions the red LED turned green. She hoped that meant that the message had been sent.

Now all she could do was wait. She nibbled idly at the dried fruit and reached out to flip through the curious little notebook. In the dark, it was difficult to read any of the faded words. She woke her phone, then wrapped the screen in a bandana. She didn't want to uncover it, fearing that it would be a beacon for her pursuers but, even through the cloth, it provided enough glowing light to see the pages. She flipped to the back to look at the notes she had seen Hoodoo taking the day before. His handwriting was neat and blocky, not at all like the sprawling, loose handwriting at the start of the notebook. She flipped back and brought the notebook closer to the glowing screen of her phone. They were written in pencil with sketches and diagrams on nearly every page. There were sketches of each of the icons from the Frenchman's map with a list of possible real world matches. She flipped past those. Next were notes on the fins of Paradise Mesa, and here she noticed that Hoodoo's blocky hand started adding notes of his own.

Just past the middle of the notebook, she stopped cold. There was a pencil line sketch of three sinuous lines that looked like a map of rivers or canyons. The writing was smeared and difficult to read in the minimal light that she had, but she thought she could make out the words "Milk Creek," and "Willis Wash." Wasn't that what Hoodoo had said was the original name of Three Goddess Canyon where he had placed the geocache? Hadn't he also said that it was unrelated to the Frenchman?

She lifted the corner of the bandana to get a little more light and thought that she could make out the words 'above,' 'canyon,' 'tumble,' and the phrases 'half way,' and 'watering hole.' In the lower corner, someone different had printed, 'Topo '67, creek westmost. Currently substantial blockage, debris 200 yards back. Creek center, strong flow. Evidence of fire pit at canyon back.' This was in ink and written in a tighter, smaller hand. She flipped to the back where Hoodoo had been taking notes about the crescents and compared it to the handwriting she found there. It looked the same; Hoodoo had known there was some connection to those canyons, and the proof was here in his own writing.

Mallory flipped to the front of the notebook turning it over and over in her hands, looking for identifying marks or dates. There was nothing. She turned back to the pages about Three Goddess Canyon and strained at them trying to make out more of the smeared pencil words.

* * *

On the shoulder of the highway, with a blanket of darkness quickly closing around them, Lynn Estes sat in a Jeep with Deputy Reyes and read off the coordinates a third time. He typed them into his dash mounted GPS and manipulated the screen, zooming in and out of the built in topographical map.

"That's rough country to cross in the dark," he said.

"Yep," Lynn said. "Question is... Are you driving? Or am I walking?"

"Can't have that, now can we?" Reyes retorted and flipped a few switches on his dashboard. The floodlights mounted on top of the Jeep bloomed into life, as did the fog lights mounted near the bumper. He pulled out onto the highway and almost immediately turned off the blacktop and into the sandy expanse of rock and scrub. "You might want to put on that seatbelt," he said, pointing the vehicle toward the looming shadow of Paradise Mesa.

CHAPTER TEN

Mallory wasn't sure when or how she had fallen asleep, but she woke suddenly and instantly. The sky was a sullen purple with a bruising of pink at the horizon but, there atop the rock where she had hidden herself, she was still in deep shadow. She looked around, sure that something had touched her and even though she saw nothing she couldn't shake the feeling that something, or someone, else was there. A pebble smacked the stone by her foot with a loud "tick," and her head snapped up looking for the source. At the top of the opposite wall, was Hoodoo, squatting at the edge, his silhouette visible against the brightening sky.

She scrambled to her feet. She had never been so thrilled to see an old hippie rock climber in her life. Above her, he waved his hands like an umpire repeatedly calling a player "safe." He put up his left hand, palm out, and placed his right index finger against his lips, still waving his right hand. *No. Stop. Be quiet.* She nodded at him and settled back to a seated position.

Hoodoo gestured to his right with an open palm then held up three fingers, he then crossed his arms making an 'X.' She cocked her head to one side, considering what he meant. A moment later she had it. *Go that way. Three intersections.*

She nodded her understanding then made her own series of gestures. Two fingers. Fingers walking across her palm. A gesture down the path towards the men she had seen. *There are two men, somewhere that way.*

He nodded, then pointed at his eyes with his index and middle fingers, then swiveled his hand in the direction they'd travelled and nodded again. *Yes, I saw them. They are that way.* He indicated 'two' with his fingers and made an 'X' with his arms, then gestured a sort of curve with his right hand. He then held up four fingers and the 'X' again. Then he folded his hands against his cheek and closed his eyes. *Two intersections in that direction, a right turn, then four more intersections. They were sleeping.*

She nodded and pointed to herself then in the direction he had indicated then put her finger to her lips. *Okay, I'll go that way, quietly.* She gathered the few belongings that were scattered around her, and used the rope to lower the two packs to the ground letting the rope drop behind them. She looked down the side of the rock that she had originally climbed, remembering where all her hand and footholds were, then looked at the other side. She'd be shielded from view if the men came up the canyon, but she couldn't see as many obvious holds on that side. She looked up at Hoodoo and pointed at her eyes as he had done, then gestured around her. *You're watching around me, right?*

He nodded and gave her the thumbs up. She returned the sign and started her descent, picking out the careful steps and holds then quickly landing on the sandy ground. She glanced behind her reassuring herself that no one had come around the corner, then up at the silhouetted form of Hoodoo high above her. She grabbed the two packs, shouldering her own, then jogged down the path. At the first intersection, she looked up to see Hoodoo leap across the void from stone to stone, nimble as a goat. At the third intersection, she looked up. Hoodoo made a series of gestures. *Turn left, travel for five intersections.* She watched him back up then leap across the gap traveling in the direction he had told her to go. He stopped long enough to make another gesture at her. *C'mon.* She jogged after him.

Before long, she was standing in front of a series of fallen stones, her progress blocked. She looked up at Hoodoo. He made a gesture with both hands, miming reaching up to grab something then pulling it down and repeating that with the other hand. Then, he pointed to the stones and made a zigzagging motion with a rising finger. *Climb up those stones.*

She shed her packs and tied a rope through the shoulder straps and the other end around her waist and began climbing. It was a straightforward climb with plenty of easy places to step and pull herself up. She was soon on the top of the rock formation, and threw her arms around Hoodoo's neck, embracing him with all the strength she had.

"Where have you been?" she whispered.

"Up here. I was headed back to you and I heard those dudes talking. I ran the other way then spotted a convenient way up. I tried to track them from up here, but I lost them, and then I lost you... It took me a while to find where I left you. Are you okay?" He broke the long hug and looked at her.

"Yeah, yeah. I hid where you found me and slept there. They walked right past me," she replied. "We need to get out of here," she whispered. "Forget the treasure, we can come back later. Do you know where we are?"

"Yeah. Mesa's that way," he indicated by extending an arm with a wide flat palm then turned his body, "that's north." He turned again; "Truck is..." he puffed out his lip, "four, maybe five miles that way?" He pointed across the forest of fins and hoodoos.

Mallory stared into the distance and tried to ignore the drop in her stomach. It all looked the same. There were no landmarks that she could recognize and it seemed to stretch forever unchanging. She may as well be adrift in the ocean. "Can you navigate it? Or should we just go back down to the floor and make our way out?"

"If we just go back down we can head towards the open desert and walk around the edge of the mesa. We'll be pretty exposed though." He scratched at his chin through his massive beard and looked back and forth between the mesa and the direction he had indicated the truck being. "Yeah. This way. We'll have to jump across the crevices for a bit." He scooped up one of the packs and started in a lope toward the truck. He quickly reached the first division between the hoodoos that they were atop, and he easily leapt over it, clearing the three-foot gap with no effort.

Mallory took the other pack and started after him but balked at the gap and stumbled, skidding to a stop at the edge. Hoodoo was already on to the next stone. He hissed back at her in a breathily whispered yell, "It's just a big step. Ignore the height."

"Easy for you to say," she muttered. She backed up to the opposite edge and took a deep breath, steeling her nerves. She broke into a jog taking two quick steps and bringing her head up. She immediately skidded to a halt and yelled, "Hoodoo!" and pointed past him.

He spun in the direction she was pointing to see another figure hoisting his self over the edge and rising onto one of the flat stones about 300 feet behind him. Mallory recognized the younger of the men she had seen the night before. Hoodoo simply stared at the young man, oddly transfixed. His body tensed in a way that she couldn't describe. He looked like a horse that had seen a snake and was trapped between the urge to stomp on it and the impulse to run away.

"Hoodoo!" she yelled at his back. "HOODOO!"

He turned toward her in a snap and started running, yelling, "Go!"

He quickly closed the gap between them and roughly took her elbow, pulling her into his momentum and towards the mesa. They reached the first gap in that direction, and she jumped without hesitation, the presence of the other man compelling her forward.

Behind them she heard the man yell, "Dad! Dad! Up here!" and to them, "Hey! There's nowhere to go! Stop!"

Hoodoo turned toward the center of the stone formations where the cracked pillars converged and became fins once again. Mallory tried her best to keep up with him but, once he released her elbow, she found herself falling behind. At over six feet tall, his long strides far outmatched her five foot six strides. She was already bone weary, hungry and thirsty without the added effort of a flat out run across rocky terrain. Ahead of her, she saw Hoodoo turn back and motion to her. She redoubled her effort to keep up, sucking in air by the lungful.

At the edge of her awareness, Mallory registered that there had been a rifle shot. She risked a glance over her shoulder at her pursuer who was much closer than she would have liked. He was still running with no sign of a gun. She didn't see anyone else. Was the other man still below and simply firing to scare them or to acknowledge that he had heard the younger man's screams? Or was he back there somewhere?

Ahead of her, she saw Hoodoo skid to a stop. The mesa had loomed up in front of them, its wooded top only slightly higher than the stone she was running across, but there was a fearfully wide gap between the two.

A memory flashed in her mind: Hoodoo had said that the last fin, the one that used to allow you to cross over onto the mesa top, had fallen. He had run toward a gap that they couldn't cross. It was a dead end. Why had he come this way? He stood on the edge near a copse of small pines, motioning at her with both hands, urging her to continue.

She huffed to a stop beside him gulping air. She tried to speak but couldn't get anything but "wha... wha..." to pass her lips.

"Stop," he said and put a hand on her shoulder. "I need you to listen. You asked me to warn you if I was about to do something you might not like. Well... here it is, the worst thing I've asked you to do: run."

She looked up into his eyes dumbly and finally managed to say, "What?"

"You have to go, and I can't stay with you anymore. I'm sorry. It's the only way I can think of to save us both. Head for the desert. Call Lynn on that thing she gave you. Stay low and close to the mesa for as long as you can."

He mind reeled and she could barely grasp what he was saying. "What about you?"

"I don't matter. Save yourself." Their eyes connected for a heartbeat and she could see the cold resolve behind his normally sleepy blue eyes. "Now! Run!" He yelled and pushed her toward the trees. He turned and ran back the way they'd come toward the man pursuing them. She watched him go, panic beating in her temples. After a few long stride he turned back to her and yelled, "Oh! And Mallory... I'm sorry!" To the man chasing them she heard him say "Justin! Justin! We don't need her! I have the map. Let her go!"

Hoodoo caught the arm of the other man, Justin she now knew, and they tussled momentarily, Justin clearly trying to continue his pursuit, Hoodoo trying to stop him. It was then that she realized that he was wearing her pack, and she was wearing his. He did have the map. It was in her bag. If the map was the thing they wanted, and Hoodoo seemed to be indicating that it was, he was in a position to give it to them. He knew this man's name, maybe he also knew why he and his father were chasing them.

They grappled like wrestlers, each gripping the other man's shoulders and trying to use their own weight and leverage to subdue the other. Justin released him and stepped back. Hoodoo's own momentum caused him to stumble forward and Justin kicked at Hoodoo's knee, moving like a striking snake. The older man went down on his side with a loud grunt. Justin leapt clear of him and his head snapped toward Mallory. His lip curled menacingly and he started running toward her again, in a swift gallop. It was another heartbeat before the panic of her brain could convince her legs to move. She scrambled at first, loose gravel and sand under her boots, but soon she was running along the edge of the fin looking desperately for a place to hide or a way to lose Justin.

She dodged into the small stand of low trees, most of which were barely the height of her own head, knowing that they wouldn't completely hide her and ducked behind the largest. Justin was close and dove at her, crashing through the small tree and ringing his arms around her waist, knocking her to the ground. They both landed with a bone-jarring crunch but, at the last possible second, she had brought her knee up so that he landed with it in his solar plexus, knocking all of the air out of him. He landed on top of her with a loud "OOF!" and a groan, pinning her between him and her own pack.

Mallory scrambled to free herself, pushing at his chest with both arms and knees before finally throwing him off of her and pushing backwards until she was able to stand again.

"I'll get you, you little..." he sputtered at her between attempts to get his breath back. She kicked at him, her heel connecting with his hip, the jarring crunch traveling up her leg. It sent him onto his back with another groan. She brought her boot down again, into his stomach. He screeched a guttural combination of breath and gurgling pain.

She ran, scanning the way ahead of her: low trees and stones, just like the rest of the lumpy surface of the fin. What was she supposed to do? Hoodoo had said to go down, but how? It was so far away and everything looked the same and she didn't know where she was. Panic began to well up and her stomach threatened to empty what little it held.

Then she spotted it. She glanced back at Justin, still on the ground clutching at his stomach, then bolted ahead praying that Justin didn't also have some sort of gun in his pocket or belt. She rapidly covered the bare surface of the fin and when she reached the sharp cut off that was the edge... she jumped into the clear air beyond.

* * *

The dusty red pickup had been parked behind a train-car-sized boulder that dwarfed it and left it in deep shadow. With a dusky morning sun providing only a weak and watery light, Lynn and Deputy Reyes had nearly driven past it. In the dark, they had been forced to take the long way through the desert. Lynn had insisted that she could navigate the treacherous Devil's Backbone in the dark, but Reyes had been unwilling to relinquish control of his Jeep, which he kept referring to as "government property," to a civilian. Lynn suspected that he was simply too scared to attempt it. Dodging it meant that they had to drive an extra 20 miles north through terrain that would have been difficult at noon, much less at midnight. It was slow going.

It had been a hawk that had drawn Lynn's attention toward the truck. Scanning the horizon, looking for the white of Hoodoo's truck, she had overlooked the red truck, which disappeared into the colored rock around them. A sudden flurry of movement, as the hawk launched itself from the rock that sheltered the truck, had pulled her eye that way. She pointed it out to Reyes, who pulled their own Jeep into position behind another large boulder several hundred yards away.

He scanned the area with his binoculars then handed them over to her. "I don't see a tent, or a fire. He could be asleep in the bed or in the cab."

"Or behind the rock," she said.

"Not a lot of cover between here and there," Reyes muttered as he pulled out his pistol, ejected the magazine, checked the contents, then shoved it back into place. He pointed with two fingers and traced a route across the desert. "Looks like there's a shallow ravine that way. It's our best shot at staying out of sight." He gave her a long appraising look, "I should make you stay here, you know."

"But you know better," she intoned.

"That I do," he sighed. "Stay low. Move quick, but don't run. Let me take the lead," he replied. They stepped out of the Jeep, both allowing the doors to slowly come to a rest, but not fully close. Lynn followed behind Reyes at a crouch. She felt silly, a little girl playing along with her old brother who was taking the game of "Cops" way too seriously. They rapidly closed the distance between the two vehicles and slid behind the rock that was shadowing the red pickup. Reyes whispered, "Stay here," and he brought the gun up to shoulder level and rounded the rock.

118

Lynn scuttled to the side of the rock and watched as he duckwalked toward the vehicle. He dropped to one knee and looked beneath the truck, then quickly stood, thrusting his gun into the bed of the truck then the open passenger window in rapid succession. He dropped his arms, returning the gun to its holster. "No one here," he called to her.

Lynn emerged from her position behind the giant boulder and narrowed her eyes at the truck. Reyes had opened the passenger door and was shuffling through the paper and other detritus that was crammed into the glove box. Lynn opened the driver door and leaned in. On the floorboard was a ripped envelope with the word "POLICE" written in bold blocky letters. She smoothed the notebook page that she found inside and quickly read through the note that Mallory Campbell had left in her own car before she and Hoodoo left for the desert. Reyes' shuffling stopped as he focused on a small slip of paper.

"Well... now I know why they broke into the girl's car." She passed the page to Reyes who took it with one hand and extended his other, passing her the car registration that he had been reading.

"I thought this was his truck. Name look familiar?" he asked her. She snatched the registration and glared at it. Reyes wasn't sure if the sound he heard her make was a curse word, a growl, or something in between, but he watched with bemusement as she slammed the truck door then repeatedly kicked it, making the same curse/noise over and over as she did so. "Hey! Hey!" He yelled at her. "You're going to crack his Bondo."

"I'm going to crack his skull!" she retorted and kicked the truck door once more. "I should have guessed he'd be involved in this..." she continued, streaming curse words in combinations that Reyes wasn't sure he had heard before.

Reyes came around the truck and leaned against the tailgate, arms crossing his chest. He waited for her steam to run out and when she sputtered to stop said, "Lynn, you want to tell me why—" he was interrupted by the distant crack of a rifle. His hand automatically went to his gun, and he stood upright, his attention strained towards the rock formations that surrounded the mesa. A few moments of silence passed, and he turned his attention back to Lynn. "Do you know that mesa well enough to guide us in?"

"Not as well as Carey," she said, "but, yeah. I know it."

"Well... the coordinates they sent with the first check-in are still about a mile and a half that way," he indicated down the mesa with a flat hand. "And the coords from the SOS were over that way," he turned about 90 degrees, "but those shots were from that way." He turned another 90 degrees. "It's a lot of land to search, and it's a maze in there. I think... I think we need back up."

CHAPTER ELEVEN

The branches of the ponderosa pine smacked into Mallory's torso with a force that she couldn't have imagined. Her horizontal momentum rapidly dissipated, and she started to gain vertical momentum as gravity reasserted its hold on her and pulled her inexorably downward. The thin branches around her rustled and cracked as she passed through them, flailing with both arms, trying to grasp something— anything— that would halt her fall. Her right hand closed on a cluster of pine needles, ripping them free, then her left hand closed on a branch that was no thicker than a shower rod. It bent with her weight redirecting her fall toward the center of the tree, near the trunk. Her fall stopped momentarily as the branch she clutched reached its maximum curve.

She hung there, feeling the rough flakes of bark rip the palm of her hand as she slipped down the branch. She swung her right arm up, closing it over her already clenched left fist and managed one shuddering breath before the branch snapped somewhere high along its arc, sending her swinging toward the trunk again. A larger branch, the thickness of her leg, slammed into her side, just below her ribs, knocking the last of her breath from her. She grunted loudly. The branch caught in her armpit and she was left dangling in midair, feet kicked for purchase that they couldn't find. She released the skinny little branch that she still clutched in her left hand and scrambled to get both arms over the thicker branch. She took a few shallow breaths, the combination of having had the air knocked from her and having her body stretched over the branch making it difficult for her to breathe deeply.

Tentatively reaching with her toes, she found another branch near her feet. The lower branch was even thicker than the one she was currently draped over. She shuffled sideways, the rough bark biting at her chest and arms, her own weight threatening to drag her the rest of the way down. Each inch brought her closer to the trunk until she was able to get her feet fully onto the other branch. She crushed her shoulder to the trunk happy to feel the reassuring solidness of it beside her. Breathe came ragged and quick and her cheeks burned with tears, but she was alive.

She looked up at the ridge she had come from. She had fallen twenty or thirty feet and was in one of the more thickly foliated sections of the tree. She could barely see the top. Was Justin still up there? Would he try to follow her? Did he think she had fallen to her death? Had Hoodoo stopped him? She couldn't be sure of anything except that she wasn't quite ready to think about Carey Estes yet, whether he was okay and what his actions meant.

She scanned down the trunk. It went down for another forty feet or so before it disappeared into darkness between two gigantic boulders. When Hoodoo had told her that the last fin had collapsed, she had always pictured something like one of those videos of a high-rise hotel being imploded, crumbling in on itself. From this angle, she thought that it must have been more like a book on a bookshelf tipping over, just falling to an angle between two other books to form a sort of 'N' shape. This tree had either taken root in between the fallen fin and its neighbor or had been crushed between. She had no idea how long it would take for a ponderosa pine to grow to this hundred-foot height.

There appeared to be an even and regular series of branches down the tree, though surveying them threatened to induce a bout of vertigo. She inclined her head and scrubbed the tears from her cheeks with her shoulders, not daring to take her hands from the branch. She picked her way down the tree, hands burned and aching, feeling shredded by the bark and needles, each stretch to find a new branch sent a lance of electricity across the ribs that had slammed into the branch. This was going to be a long climb.

She had never considered herself to be a short person, but she must be, she thought. Each step down felt slightly longer than the last, and soon an ache in her thighs began to echo the ache in her hands and ribs. With about fifteen feet left, she ran out of branches.

From here, it was much easier to see that the tree continued into the crevice between the fallen fin and the wall. Below her was the rounded edge of the fin. On one side, it would be a short, sharp descent into the terrifying darkness where the tree was rooted. The other side of the fin angled off like the world's widest playground slide. She could see a few places where she might be able to gain a footing but, if she missed, she could potentially slide all the way to the bottom, which looked like a pile of debris left by the collapse. A fall to either side would end in disaster meaning she couldn't simply jump and hope for the best.

One thing drew her clear attention though: the mesa wall. At the bottom of the slide the mesa wall was a mosaic of brilliant greens. It appeared to be covered in moss and other close growing plants and that meant one thing: water. She desperately needed water, and a morning of running, jumping, and climbing had not made that any better.

She wrestled the pack off of one shoulder, careful not to over balance, and tried to reach into the top of Hoodoo's pack. They had abandoned most of the climbing gear back at the granary, but there was at least one length of rope left. She dug into the pack, pushing spare clothing to the side until she felt the bundle of rope and started to pull at it. One of the packets of freeze-dried food pulled free along with the rope, and she watched it spin down to the ground, then bounce once and slide down the long slope toward the mesa wall.

With slow, deliberate motions she pulled the shoulder strap of the pack back into place, and looped the rope around the tree, the loose ends falling to the ground. She had no harness or other equipment to guide her descent, but at least the rope would prevent her from following the food packet. At least she hoped so.

She laughed sharply to herself, realizing that she probably wouldn't have attempted what she was about to do a few days ago. Not before Hoodoo's little crash course in canyoneering. She exhaled, scooted off the last branch, and felt the rope go taut, taking her weight. A few seconds later and she was on the ground. She peered down into the crevice and could see that the gigantic tree extended for at least another ten feet before the darkness completely enclosed it and she could no longer see the trunk.

Pulling the rope free of the branch, she looped it around the trunk and threw the ends down the face of the slope. The rope was 60 meters, about 200 feet, so doubled as she had seen Hoodoo do, it fell short of the end of the slope by about a third. She could tie the rope off, but that would mean abandoning it, and it was the last rope she had. She had to risk crossing the last stretch without a safety line.

Above her, on the ridge she had leapt off, she could see no one. Neither Hoodoo, Justin, nor the mysterious third man, Justin's father she remembered, could be seen. She knew she wasn't exactly "alone" on the mesa, but she was most definitely on her own at this point.

Digging through Hoodoo's pack, she found a bandana and ripped it into two oblong rectangles that she could wrap around her raw palms. Blood welled in tiny crimson beads from the scrapes and lashes that crisscrossed her palms. Maybe there would be enough water below that she could use some to wash her wounds. She hoped so. Hoisting the pack, she started to step backward down the slope. It was steep, she estimated that it must be somewhere between 30 and 45 degrees, and slick, with a few ridges here and there, but she'd mostly be relying on the rubber lugs of her hiking boots to keep herself upright.

By the time she was halfway down the slope, her calves and hamstrings burned from the angle of the descent and the effort; her already dry mouth was starting to feel sticky and her tongue felt thick.

Soon the rope ran out. She estimated that there was another 50 feet until she reached the bottom of the slope, and the pile of loose gravel and rock that had collected between the fallen fin and the mesa wall. She scanned over her shoulder as best she could, looking for handholds and footholds that she could use to traverse the last length. There didn't appear to be much, but she thought she saw a few places. She released one side of the rope, and pulled the other through her shoulder strap, knotting it loosely. Her hands would be free, and she could simply allow the length of rope to pull behind her.

Feeling below her for a toehold, she felt her boot connect with a thin ridge of rock and took a step. Her already raw fingers dug into the surface of the stone trying to find something to grip.

Three more steps raised her confidence levels and left her feeling like Andrew Garfield in his Spider-Man suit, scaling a wall. She stepped back again, and immediately knew that she had made a bad choice. Her boot connected with a lip of rock but, when she shifted her weight to that leg, she felt the rock slide and her foot went with it. With one leg straight back, the other collapsed, splaying sideways, and she landed on the rock, face first, a grunt leaving her. Her center of gravity shifted sideways as the weight of her pack dragged her over and she watched herself slide inexorably down the slope as if she were outside her own body. Her arms and legs scrambled, but the pack prevented her from getting onto her back, leaving her sliding down the face of the fin on her side, gaining speed all the while.

She snapped back into her body as she felt her legs hit the debris pile, and she came almost into a standing position. The ungainly and abrupt landing meant that she immediately toppled backward again, landing hard on the pack and sliding further down the loose scree. She came to rest about 50 feet later, and lay still where she landed, feeling a shower of gravel and small stones landing around her, bouncing off her face and sides.

Mallory moaned and tried to sit up, but a wave of dizziness sent her down again. She reached up slowly and pulled the shoulder straps of the pack away, disconnecting herself from the dead weight, and rolled roughly onto her side. She was sure it was one of the less graceful moments of her life.

Slowly sitting up, she felt for any new pain. Her side felt like she'd been in a fight with a cheese grater, and she was sure that she'd have a spectacular case of road rash if she could stand to lift her shirt. Otherwise, her shredded hands and bruised ribs were still at the forefront of her list of complaints. That was a good thing she supposed.

The pack was almost as worse for wear as she was. The side was shredded, with multiple holes and rips. Miraculously she had kept hold of the rope, which now puddled in a tangle near her feet, the end trailing off across the loose scree that she had just bounced across. Digging into one of the larger holes in the pack, she pulled out the t-shirt with the map printed on the front. She swiped it across her face in an attempt to remove the worst of the dust and grit that had collected there. The pack was going to need some help if it was going to continue fulfilling its function. She pulled in the rest of the rope and used it to lash the map t-shirt around the ripped side. Hopefully that would hold everything inside.

Standing wasn't easy, and she had to drag the pack behind her rather than wearing it on her back. She was just too tired to lift it. Picking her way across the loose scree was slow going but a turned ankle was the last thing she needed. At the end was the pot of gold: water. As she got closer, she could smell it. In a dry, dusty desert the water smelled like heaven: green and mossy, like rain. From this angle, she could see that the wall of the mesa had a scooped shape, a deep irregular semi-dome cut into the rock by water. The opposing face of the fin bore the other half of the dome. Millions of years of water and wind had eaten away at both formations creating a weakness in the fin, and eventually causing it to fall, separating the two halves like a broken open clamshell. A curtain of water fell in thin steams, filling the open front of the little cave like strands of diamonds. Inside, the water collected into a small pool, a little more than a foot deep, with sharp vertical sides like a giant pot. At the bottom of the pool, she could see another pot-shaped hole, smaller, but another foot or so deep. The pool, in turn, spilled over into a thin stream that sparkled away toward the desert. The air was thick with humidity and fragrant with plant life. The floor of the cave was small gravel, like a manicured rock garden.

Mallory stepped through the curtain of water into the green paradise. The pool in the center of the cavern glittered so blue and cool that she wanted to cry. She dropped the bag and knelt beside the pool, sticking her face into the water and drinking deeply. Words like "giardia" and "cryptosporidium" bubbled up in the back of her brain, but she decided that dehydration and being chased by people with guns were more important concerns at the moment.

It was amazing how much better she felt after even a little water, and she lay back on the loose stone suddenly feeling safe and content. All she wanted was to sleep and rest, but it only lasted a few brief moments before reality crashed into her mind and she pulled herself upright, groaning at her various aches. She needed to get down to the desert and see if she could get help, or get away, but she also needed water, and food, and to take care of her injuries. She'd rapidly be useless in the desert if she tried to cross it tired, hungry, thirsty, and bleeding. It would only take an hour or so to get herself into a reasonable shape.

The next few minutes were filled with activity. Filling a pot and setting it to boil, then moving downstream and washing the blood and grit out of the wounds on her hands. She shed her shirt, and dabbed the wet handkerchiefs from her hands at the rash she found along her side, wincing a little. She'd certainly left some skin on the slope. At the pool, she filled two water bottles and the water bladder that was internal to the pack.

There was a flurry of black feathers and a gigantic raven landed sending dust away in a cloud. It cocked its head to one side and croaked brashly at her, "Cr-r-r-ruck."

"Well," she croaked back, voice still harsh and dry sounding, "is that you Huginn? Where's your partner?"

"Cr-ruck?" the raven replied.

"Better than no company at all I guess," she muttered and moved back into the cave, picking her way carefully so that she didn't jostle any of her numerous bumps and scrapes. "I'll try to ignore any ominous connotations you being here might have." The raven hopped behind her, undeterred by the dripping water, and took a perch on a lumpy white rock near the opening, carefully watching her every move. "Time for some breakfast!" she told the bird, and slowly lowered herself onto the loose gravel, folding her legs beneath her.

After sorting through the options, she dropped some freeze-dried beef stroganoff into the boiling water and dove deeper into Hoodoo's pack. A first aid bag yielded some familiar ruddy-red ibuprofen tablets that she quickly swallowed and an ointment that she liberally applied to her ribs and palms. She pulled on one of Hoodoo's shirts, which was a bit large, but not overwhelmingly so, and was at least clean and not spattered with blood. In a small pouch she found an odd device, about a foot long, shaped like a stake or an icicle. She popped a cover from the base and found what looked like a fluorescent bulb underneath. She looked again at the base and found the words "UV Sterilizer." She reached for one of the water bottles. There was a threaded flange around the long bulb of the sterilizer that was the perfect size to screw onto the mouth of the water bottle, replacing the lid. She inserted the bulb into the water, screwed it into place and depressed the switch on the top. The long thin bulb that was now immersed in the water emitted a soft blue glow, barely perceptible in the daylight. She waited a few minutes and removed the sterilizer.

"Better than giardia," she said to the raven, and repeated the sterilization process on the second bottle. She returned to her digging in the pack and in another packet she found purification tablets that she dropped into the water bladder. "I might be lost, but I'll be hydrated for a while."

To one side of the pack, she spotted the little leather notebook and pried it free. It had a fresh scrape along the front cover, having taken some of the damage of her slide, though it was no worse than the wear that was already on the little book. She laid the book open on her lap and slowly flipped through it as she tenderly ate the steaming stroganoff.

"What do you make of this?" she said aloud, talking to the bird she supposed.

"C-r-r-r-ruck-uck!"

"Mmm. Listen, Hugh... Can I call you Hugh? Huginn is kind of a mouthful," she slid open a freezer bag full of cashews and tossed a small handful toward the large black bird.

"Cuck!!" it called, hopping eagerly onto the cashews.

"Hugh it is. Here's what we know, Hugh. Hoodoo lied to me about not knowing of a connection between those canyons and the Frenchman. He's got a whole notebook here about the guy, and I'm pretty sure this is a map of the canyons." She thumped the page with the back of her hand.

"Crr-r-ruck! Cuck!" the bird called.

"Yep. Pretty incriminating," she said, and tossed a few more nuts toward him. "He also seems to know who these guys with the guns are. At least one of them."

"Cu-rrk!"

"Well, that's a pretty nasty thing to call him, but right now I'm inclined to agree. He's run off alone twice now, 'scouting' as he called it. Do you think he could have been meeting with them? He told that Justin boy that 'we don't need her.' He said, 'we.'" She didn't like that thought, because it led to conclusions that she wasn't comfortable with.

"Crawk?" Hugh asked, then went back to pecking in the pea-sized gravel, searching for any nuts he might have overlooked.

She tossed a few more nuts toward the bird. "Does that mean you've seen him with them? Or that I'm being silly? Or are you saving that information for Odin?" She laughed softly to herself.

"Crawk?" he asked again.

"Just give it to me straight. Is Hoodoo working with those guys?"

"Cak! Cak! Cak!"

"I hope you're right," she said. "But I still kinda think he might be."

"Cuck! Cuck! Craw!"

"I know. It's harsh. But lately I've had some experience with... let's just call them father figures that turned out to be not so trustworthy." She blew air through her lips in a frustrated gesture and slumped back, dropping the camping spoon into the little bowl of stroganoff. "Maybe I'm letting my disappointment in Toller color my conclusions on Hoodoo, but I've had about all I can take of men who have secret agendas."

She reached out absently and flipped another page in the little notebook. The next page was dominated by a drawing of a thundercloud. Pulling the backpack closer, she flipped it over so that she could see the image of the Frenchman's map printed on the shirt she had lashed to the outside. She pulled at the rope a bit so that she could see the map a little better. The thundercloud was the next to last symbol. After that was the big cartoonish eye shape that Hoodoo had said represented the mesa itself. She turned the page to find that image in the notebook. On the left, in the creaky pencil line, was a copy of the mesa drawing: a roughly circular shape with a wavering edge that looked like a very rough map of an island. Off-center toward the southeastern quadrant of the shape was another rough circle. Hoodoo had said that this represented the "Frenchman's Eye," up above on the mesa.

Beside the drawing, the person writing in pencil had scratched, "Depth: 276. Broken wench arm 2 o'clock? Wagon wheel and chain 40 feet SSW." On the opposite page, Hoodoo's handwriting had a small paragraph: *"Cabin of local material, stone and wood scavenged. Only fasteners and stove brought in. Lowered from wench?"* Along the bottom of the page, in a faded ink, was what Mallory thought might be a third handwriting. It said simply: "Nothing there." She flipped idly through the book looking for other examples of the third hand but saw none.

"Awk! Cra!" called Hugh, as he flapped the few feet to the edge of the pool. He bent and stuck his beak into the cool water, and Mallory exhaled a small laugh.

"A nice drink by the pool, huh? A bird after my own..." her voice trailed off, and her eyes traced the outline of the pool, then fell at the dark shape of the indentation at the bottom. She set the bowl aside and got quickly to her feet, moving around the pool.

"Cr-r-r-r-rawk!" Hugh croaked at her, startled by her sudden movement, and he fluttered back to his white rock perch by the opening of the cave.

Mallory oriented her body, then brought the notebook up and flipped back to the page about the mesa. She compared the shape of the pool to the shape drawn there. The outline of the mesa in the book was a rough match for the outline of the pool, and the position of the "Frenchman's Eye" echoed the position of the deeper indention at the bottom of the pool.

"As above, so below. Right, Hugh?"

She excitedly dug into her pocket and fished out her phone. She uttered a small curse when she saw that at some point in her adventures this morning, she had cracked the screen. A jagged lightning bolt crossed from top to bottom. It still powered on though, and she swiped through photos, passing by the photos she had taken of the sherd she had found, and inwardly shuddering at the reminder that the real world was still going on without her. She was also reminded that this was the only proof she had of the sherd and, if the phone were to be damaged beyond repair, that proof would be lost. She'd have nothing with which to confront Toller. Of course, that all also relied on her actually surviving this whole experience and getting back to civilization.

She arrived at the photos she had taken of the second half of the map, what she thought of as "her" half, and found the photo of the three goddess figures: one with a circle behind its head, one with multiple arms, and one with a spiral beside it, like a long curly tail. She re-read the instructions beside those figures: 'Pray to the mother. See as the cat. Weave as the spider.'

"All right, Hugh. The granary had this figure with the halo drawn on it. Have you seen this figure with the tail somewhere around here?" She turned the phone up toward the bird, as if to show him the image, and looked again at the lumpy white rock where it was sitting. From this different angle, it looked remarkably like a large white cat, curled up but with its head upright. It even had two stubby ears.

"I'll be," she breathed. "Hello there, Lady Bast. Welcome to the party. Have you met Hugh? Okay. Okay. Clearly this is the last stop on the map if you come from the bottom. What next? C'mon Bast! What's my next step?" She moved around the circumference of the cave, her feet crunching on the gravel floor, muttering, "Just one right thing." The bird seemed to have no further input on the problem but remained atop the cat-shaped rock watching her. "Hugh? Any input here?"

She scanned the walls and the pool looking for anything out of the ordinary. The only thing that stood out to her was toward the center back of the cave: a deeper cut into the wall. It was low, about 18 inches off the floor of the cave, but looked as though it went deeply into the wall. She went back to the pack and pulled out a headlamp clicked it on, and pointed the beam into the dark, low crevice. It went back into the mesa wall for a dozen feet or more, like a crawlspace beneath an enormous house, the light of the headlamp falling away into darkness again before she saw a back to the space.

"Is this what he means by seeing 'as a cat?' Seeing in the dark?" She shuffled out of the crevice and sat up. "Hugh? Advice? Bast?"

The bird merely cocked its head to the side and stared toward her. Hugh's head bobbed, and he fluttered his wings but remained in place.

"Great. Now's the perfect time to go silent on me," she muttered at him. "You guys are no help at all."

He folded his wings and hopped sideways, attention suddenly outside the cave rather than directed at her. Mallory narrowed her eyes trying to figure out what had drawn his attention. She stepped to the front of the cave, the shimmery curtain of water fell before her, but she didn't step through it. The bird's attention remained focused on the world on the other side of the curtain of water. He lowered his head and scanned in front of them. "Crawk!" he barked gutturally.

It was then that Mallory heard it: there were voices echoing through the valley. She couldn't make out individual words, but there was a rhythmic quality to the utterances. Then she heard a loud scraping sound, like something heavy being dragged across concrete. It stopped and there was silence for a moment. She heard the voices again, three quick syllables, then the sound of the stone moving. Her mind pieced it all together; it was the sound of someone counting, followed by people moving a stone. Where was it coming from?

She stepped out of the cave and scanned up and down the face of the fin, the face of the mesa wall, toward both ends of the valley, but saw no one. Hugh fluttered behind her, startling her momentarily, and he glided over to a large boulder at the base of the fin amongst the small scree and other debris.

She heard the rhythmic chant again, sure this time that she could make out the words "One! Two! Three!"

Hugh launched off the rock he had been sitting on with a loud "CR-R-R-RAWK!" that echoed through the valley. The rock shifted almost imperceptibly, and a small clatter of loose gravel slid away from its base.

Mallory's heart leapt into her mouth. She backed into the cave, splashing across the small stream and through the curtain of falling drops, unable to take her eyes off the rock. The cold water on her neck snapped her back to reality and she scrambled around the cave, gathering everything she had been using and shoving it into the pack with no regard for order or space. How had she used so many things? She tied the pack closed, as well as she could, and ran back to the cave opening. Her choices were to try to go up the valley toward the interior of the fins or down toward the desert. Either was fully exposed. If the men moved the rock and created a hole that they could climb through, they'd almost immediately be able to see her. How long would it take for them to accomplish that?

She looked back into the cave and spotted the low crevice at the back, the crawlspace. She ran to it and shoved the pack ahead of her, crawling in behind it. "Please God, don't let there be snakes back here," she whispered. Behind her she heard a loud crunch, followed by a rushing noise that she realized was a rockslide. Loud whooping voices filled the canyon. They had made it through.

CHAPTER TWELVE

Deputy Alejandro Reyes clicked his radio handset back into the holster on the dash of his Jeep and watched Lynn Estes pace back and forth in front of the truck. "Hoo boy," he said in deep exhalation. "This is going to go over like a lead balloon." He stepped out of the truck. Lynn stopped in mid stride and turned sharply to him, her arms crossed across her chest. "They're sending backup, but we gotta wait," Reyes said.

"And why is that?" she said, icily.

"The girl called her brother. Told him to wait 72 hours before he went to their parents--"

"We know this!" Lynn barked, and her left hand shot out and smacked the hood of the Jeep.

Reyes' eyes went to the point on the Jeep that she had hit and remained there for a long second, then swiveled up to meet hers, though his head never moved. "Yes... but the parents also caught wind of some trouble she got into down in Arizona and forced the brother to tell them what he knew."

"What kind of trouble? Police trouble?"

"Well... I admit it didn't sound like much to me. She walked off some summer job down there." He shrugged. "I don't know. Sounds like the parents were making a big deal out of it. Boy spilled the beans sometime last night, and the parents have been calling every phone number they could find on the Garfield County website since then." He scrubbed his palm across his close-cropped hair.

"And someone finally answered?" She kicked a rock and sent it skittering across the dirt.

"Yep. And when they made the connection between the girl's name and the report I filed this morning..." He held up his hands in a gesture of surrender.

"What do they want you to do?" Lynn asked, knowing that this was rapidly spinning away from her.

"Since I'm already out here, they've put me on point. I'm to guard the truck and make sure no one tries to leave. They have a chopper on the way, but it's coming from the rescue station down at Zion. It's going to be a bit." He braced himself for her inevitable outburst. Lynn's head was cocked so that her ear was near her shoulder. Her head slowly rocked to the other side, her flat eyes never leaving the deputy's. She stood silently until Reyes began to feel uncomfortable.

"Fine," she said finally, surprising him. "You enjoy your little camp out... I'm going into the mesa." She turned toward the back of the Jeep, a look of determination on her face.

"Lynn. Lynn..." Reyes said, hustling to follow her to the back of the Jeep where she started fumbling with the rear door, trying to open the storage compartment where they had stowed packs and supplies. "Lynn, you can't open that," he said.

"The hell I can't!" she retorted, yanking on the handle. She stepped back and raised a foot as if to kick the door and he took a quick step between her and the Jeep.

"Lynn," he said sternly, "you ain't gonna kick my Jeep. You can't open it because it's locked. It's always locked! We keep guns in there. You can't open it without a key!" Her foot went down slowly and casually making it clear that she was lowering it because she wanted to, not because he had told her to. She stepped back, crossing her arms. He tried to make his voice as comforting as he could manage. "We'll get in the mesa. We just have to wait for backup now. Okay?"

Lynn's face crumpled momentarily, as if she were about to cry, but her expression solidified, and she looked into his face with determination. "You don't get it, do you? You don't get exactly who that is that's out there shooting at my husband. Most of the town sees him as some harmless old coot living out some prospector fantasy in the desert, but he's not. He's just not."

"And what is he then?"

She fixed him with a look that said she knew she was about to tell him something that he wasn't going to believe. "He's one of the most evil men that's ever walked."

Reyes guffawed. "Hiram?"

"Yeah," she said firmly, and crossed her arms. "Hiram. Trust me. I know. We know."

"Okay." He huffed a heavy breath and scrubbed his palm across his scalp. She had already come to recognize this as a compulsory "tell" that meant he didn't want to say whatever the next sentence was. "In which case I really can't let you go in there."

Lynn kicked the bumper of the Jeep, connecting hard enough to rock the vehicle. Reyes glared at her and produced a white handkerchief from seemingly nowhere, kneeling to brush any errant dust from the bumper. When he was satisfied that the truck was unharmed, he stood slowly.

"Please don't make me handcuff you in the back seat," he said, with a slow deliberateness.

Lynn's shoulders dropped, and her fists unclenched with a sigh. "Sorry."

"The chopper is coming. If they are on top of the mesa, we'll find them fast."

"And if they are between the fins?" she asked.

"There are heat vision cameras and all sorts of things. We'll find them."

"Alex. Please," she pleaded.

"We'll find them," he said and dropped his large hand awkwardly onto her shoulder in a gesture that seemed like a close approximation of comforting someone.

She looked at his hand then up into his eyes. "You're better at showing that you care about this Jeep than you are with people," she said. "You should work on that."

"I'll take a seminar as soon as we get back to civilization," he said, and sniffed a short laugh.

* * *

Mallory shifted her position by millimeters, trying not to make a sound. She had donned a headlamp and crept into the crevice until she was sure that she couldn't be seen from below the edge of the cave where the pool was. She'd listened to the three men clear a hole large enough to climb through and, as soon as she could clearly hear their voices, she pushed deeper into the crevice until she didn't think she could be seen by a casual observer. She had reoriented herself so that she could see into the cave and watch the three men, but that was 20 minutes ago and now she could feel every pebble and stone that was under her, especially the ones that poked into the bruises and scrapes on her ribs. She pushed up on her hands, wincing as the rock grated on her palms. Trading one pain for another, she supposed.

She settled onto her chest and looked back into the cave. From her vantage point, she could see all three of the men, Hoodoo, Justin, and the older man, as they crested the rise, and stepped through the shimmering beads of the falling water. She felt like a small child hiding under an enormous bed and spying on her parents.

"So, what next?" the older man said. "The thundercloud was on the backside of that fallen rock, so the final symbol should be here somewhere, right?"

She could see the boots and legs of the men. Once they were inside the cave she couldn't see much above their hips. Hoodoo squatted by the pool and scooped a handful of the cool water into his mouth while Justin was kicking at rocks, and the older man, clad in cowboy boots rather than the hiking boots that the other two wore, paced the circumference of the cave.

She heard Hoodoo say, "It may not be as easy as just finding the next symbol Uncle Hiram." Mallory felt the breath go out of her. Uncle? This man was Hoodoo's uncle? Which made Justin, what? His cousin? Why was Hoodoo's uncle chasing them? If they were his family would that mean that he really was helping them? As much as she had hated herself for doubting Hoodoo's intentions a lump came to her throat and she felt her mouth harden to a thin line. Outside, Hoodoo's voice continued, "We had to climb all over that wall at the Mary shaped hoodoo to get what we needed. If my Daddy was reading the map right..."

Hiram's raised voice cut Hoodoo off mid-sentence, "Your Daddy wasn't right about anything! I found that trail! I figured out how to get across the top of those fins! ME! Your Daddy didn't do nothing but try and jump my claim!" He had closed the space between him and Hoodoo; it appeared to Mallory the two men were standing face-to-face. Hoodoo's left foot scooted back a bit as if he were bracing himself against a shove.

"You followed Daddy around like hound dog. How is it you figured out anything?" Hoodoo yelled. Mallory heard a sound like wet laundry being dropped on concrete and suddenly Hoodoo was lying on the ground clutching his chin. Hiram stepped over Hoodoo and used the toe of his boot to press Hoodoo's shoulder to the ground.

"Let's get this straight once and for all," Hiram intoned, with a coldly deliberate voice. "Me and your Daddy climbed all over this mesa looking for this treasure, but then you were born, and he got soft. I figured out the map. I found the trail. When I had my legal troubles your Daddy took all that work and tried to claim it with that little forgery of a notebook he carried everywhere." Mallory found her hand involuntarily moving toward the pack where she knew the little leather notebook to be nestled. Was the pencil writing Hoodoo's father?

Hoodoo swatted at Hiram's leg knocking the booted foot off his shoulder. "And when you got out of jail and realized how close Daddy was to finally making the find, you made sure he had an accident on the trail!" Hoodoo's strained voice echoed in the crevice where Mallory was hidden. Hiram dropped to his knees beside Hoodoo, one knee landing squarely on his stomach and forcing his breath from him in a startling 'OOF!' noise. Hiram brought his face to Hoodoo's pressing their noses together.

"I wish I had killed your Daddy," he said. "But it ain't my fault he didn't know how to set an anchor so he doesn't fall off a mountain. Talk to me like that again, and I'll throw you off the mountain, and you can join him. AND that girl." The terrifying man stood and stalked toward the pool.

Hoodoo rolled onto one elbow working his jaw with the other hand as if he were trying to shove it back into place. He stopped, and his eyes narrowed. He reached forward and brushed some of the gravel away then lifted a shiny silver strip of plastic. Mallory recognized it as the top of the foil bag that had held her freeze-dried meal of stroganoff. Based on the look on his face, Hoodoo recognized it as well. He slowly turned his head, scanning the cave. Was he looking for her? If he spotted her would he tell Hiram and Justin that she was there?

"Pa!" Justin's voice rang out, "Here!" He was standing very close to the point where Mallory had entered the crevice. A clump of green plant life fell at his feet, then another. He was yanking the plants and moss from the wall.

"I'll be," Hiram said, approaching his son's position. "Looks like one of them drawings on the new part of the map. Maybe the cat-woman!" There was a wet pop, which Mallory though must be Hiram congenially slapping his son's back. So, Hiram had seen her half of the map at some point. She wondered if it was before or after she and Hoodoo were separated.

"Looks like it don't matter where the last symbol is. We found the second goddess," Hiram brayed loudly.

Though she couldn't see it, Mallory knew that they had uncovered a petroglyph, most likely the female figure with the spiraling tail.

"Carey," Hiram's harsh voice filled the space, "what did the map say about this one?"

"See as the cat..." Hoodoo replied absently, as if he were considering the meaning of the phrase himself.

"Cats see in the dark," Justin offered, hopefully.

"Long wait 'til dark," Hiram mused grumpily.

"I think he means the tin," Hoodoo said, seeming to have made a decision. He lay back putting his head and shoulders into the gravel.

"The tin? That thing the Frenchman had? With the quartz? How does that help you see in the dark?" Justin asked dismissively, the scent of the treasure must have felt close to him.

"I think it was a lantern shield," Hoodoo said, and slowly turned his head so that he was peering directly into the crevice: directly at her. Could he possibly know she was there? Her mind raced. Had he guessed she was there? "It was there to direct the lantern light through the quartz."

"Right. Like a flashlight. Just like I said," Justin concluded dully and started digging in a pack that he had dropped by the entrance.

Hoodoo continued to stare into the crevice where she was hidden, his eyes dancing back and forth, scanning the darkness. A glimmer of a mischievous smile crossed his face and he said in a small, quiet voice, "Like a prism."

Neither Justin nor Hiram reacted. Mallory wasn't even sure they had heard him, but her mind raced. If the quartz stone was a prism, and the tin blocked some of the light... could it have been arranged to let *some* light through? A specific color or wavelength? Justin returned with the flashlights, interrupted her thoughts.

"So, we can see in the dark... what are we looking for? And where is the dark?" Justin said.

Hiram interrupted him, "Petroglyph of the goddess marked the way at the granary, according to Carey, here. Should be the same." He dropped to his knee and suddenly his lined face was visible at the opening of the crevice. His dark hair, shot through with gray, seemed a bit too long for his face and hung lankly around his head. He looked mean, all gristle and beard bristles, the kind of man she'd expect to see kick a dog. "Bring me one o'them lights. Looks plenty dark back there," he growled.

Mallory's guts clenched and her mind warred with only two options: move or stay still. Either seemed like an impossibly bad choice. She counted Justin's footsteps as he approached his father and lowered a flashlight into his hand. Hiram fumbled with the switch, trying to get it on.

With a crunching sound Hoodoo pushed himself up in a seated position and said to Hiram's back, "Well... Daddy wouldn't have..."

The flashlight dropped as Hiram stood and rounded on Hoodoo, Justin followed suit and all three voices rose in anger. Gravel crunched as the men shoved one another and churned in a small fighting mass. Mallory used the cover of the noise to scoot back deeper into the crevice, dragging the backpack with her. She bumped her head on the stone ceiling and felt it scrape the small of her back. It seemed to be getting lower; was she reaching the end? She scooted again but suddenly realized that she didn't feel the ceiling above her shoulders any longer. She cautiously raised her head and then reached up with a flat palm. There was nothing. The ceiling was significantly higher here. Cautiously she came up on her knees, still feeling for a ceiling that no longer seemed to be there.

She ducked quickly and looked back out into the cave where the men were. The physical tussling seemed to have stopped, but the men were still engaged in a verbal fight. She raised her head and snapped on the headlamp. In the blooming circle of light she found that there was an opening above her, one that went higher than the beam her headlamp

142

was throwing. She stood and realized that the ceiling of the crevice here became the floor of a cavern, large and open. She grabbed her pack and hoisted herself up onto the ledge, just as she did she saw the beam of a flashlight play across the ground where she had just been lying; the men were entering the crevice.

Being careful that her light did not shine down into the hole she had just emerged from, Mallory scanned the room. It was about the size of large hotel room with crenulated sandstone walls of orange and pink, just like the outside of the mesa. A few large boulders littered the floor. Across the room, there were three deep recesses. She could see the center one most clearly, and it appeared to extend deeper into the mesa, like a tunnel.

Voices pulled her attention back to the hole in the floor. At least one of them was close. Mallory scuttled behind the largest of the boulders and tried to hide herself as best she could. When she was comfortable, she snapped the headlamp off plunging her into the deepest darkness that she had ever experienced. It was like lying in a coffin. Her brain struggled to find light, or anything visual, but found nothing but the profoundest black. She lay there in the dark listening to the growing sound of the men grunting as they crawled through the dark beneath her, the sound growing louder and closer every moment. She thought she could see a light now as well, though maybe it was just a failure of her brain.

"Hey!" she heard a voice proclaim. Justin, or Hoodoo? Mallory was sure now that she could see light coming from the hole she had climbed through. "There's a... tunnel... or..." she recognized the voice as Justin, the sound of it filling the cavern, along with his light. She withdrew into herself trying to be as small and as invisible as she could be.

There were a series of scrapes and grunts as the three men hauled themselves up into the cavern and their lights washed the walls filling all the corners. She listened as they milled about, scuffing their boots on the stone, examining the corners of the space. It suddenly felt small and crowded. How could they not see her?

"Three tunnels," grunted Hiram. "No markings that I can see." It must be his light that she could see sweeping the ceiling.

"No tracks or prints," said Hoodoo. "I don't think there's been anyone in here in decades."

"Which one would a cat take, I guess is the question. Justin, check that one. Carey, down there." Hiram's tone brooked no disagreement, and invited no debate.

The light and sound receded as the men stalked into the tunnels, plunging Mallory back into silence and the all-enclosing dark. It was only moments before rapid footfalls announced someone's return to the main cavern in a rush.

"Tunnel closes off after about...." Justin's voice trailed off when he realized that he was alone in the cavern. She listened to him shuffling back and forth, sand and gravel crunching beneath his boots. The hazy circle of his headlamp moved around the walls. He shuffled to the corner of the space, kicking a stone that clattered to a rest by her foot. She watched his light dip to the floor and swing back and forth. He was examining the area behind the boulders! He stood and moved, dipping his head behind another boulder, moving closer to her.

"Boy!" Hiram's voice suddenly boomed through the room causing Mallory to flinch. Justin's light swung up abruptly momentarily lighting the area where she was hiding, but he didn't seem to notice. "Find anything?"

"Blocked after about 100 yards," Justin replied, crunching his way to his dad's side. They were on the left side of the room. Justin must have gone into the left-most tunnel, and Hiram into the center.

"Yeah? Well, you missed a side tunnel because mine looped into yours and led me back here!" She heard a dry smack that sounded like Hiram hitting Justin. "C'mon!" he commanded. Both of their lights swung toward the right side of the room, into the last tunnel the one that Hiram had sent Hoodoo into, presumably. It was dark once again and she listened to their steps retreat. When everything was silent she released a breath she hadn't realized that she was holding. Several minutes passed, and no one returned to the cavern. The tunnel must extend away from her for quite a distance.

She considered what Hoodoo may have been trying to tell her back at the pool. His quiet whisper, "Like a prism," floated around in her mind. She felt silly now for doubting him, for thinking that he could have betrayed her so easily. She still had some questions about why he had kept his dad's involvement in this a secret, but that could wait.

"Okay," she whispered to herself, "one right thing." What would it mean if the quartz crystal that the Frenchman had with him when he died was actually a prism? And not only a prism, but a prism mounted to a lantern shield? If it were designed to allow only a specific wavelength through, was there something in the room that would react to that?

She sat up and listened intently to the darkness. There was no sound, no evidence that the men were headed back her direction. She tentatively reached up and clicked on the headlamp that she was wearing. The room flared into light and she shielded her eyes to prevent being blinded by the loss of night vision. When she thought it was safe, she took a quick survey of the walls and saw nothing. She clicked a switch on the headlamp and the LEDs switched to red. She swung her head from side-to-side, but still saw nothing. Another press of the switch shifted the LEDs to blue but provided no further clarity. If she had her own pack, she would have a black light, which she kept in her geocaching supplies. Some geocaches used ultraviolet inks to provide clues, and the black light had also been helpful during night caches: geocaches intended to be done after dark.

The thought of ultraviolet ink tickled something in her brain. Would Tevbaugh have known about fluorescence? She concentrated trying to remember anything she had ever read or heard about it. The Chinese had been using fluorescence when western civilization was still focused around the

Mediterranean. She thought she remembered something about the Aztec using a fluorescent tincture as a medicine, and the fluorescent qualities of quinine were discovered in the 1600's. When had fluorescent minerals been discovered? She wasn't sure, but it didn't matter, really. Hoodoo had her black light.

She sat down on a boulder and looked around for her pack hoping for a drink of water.

Wait. Water. That was it! The idea that had been tumbling half-formed in her mind clicked into place. She pulled the pack to her and fished inside for the water bottle, and then for the UV water purifier that she had used by the pool. She clicked it on and inserted it into the water screwing its mount onto the mouth of the bottle. The water lit up with bluish light and radiated through the clear plastic of the bottle. She clicked off her headlamp and held the bottle aloft.

Above the central tunnel was a shimmering blue arrow.

CHAPTER THIRTEEN

Mallory stood between the tunnel and the hole in the floor as an internal debate warred. The smart move would be to crawl back out to the cave where the pool of fresh water had been, then down the side of the mesa to escape. Instead, she was staring down the mouth of a dark tunnel with a shimmering blue arrow pointing into it. Tevbaugh had the soul of a geocacher-- that was certain. He knew exactly how to tempt her to follow him down the rabbit hole and possibly into further danger. Whatever her decision she needed to move *now*. They could be back any second. The two tunnels she had listened to them explore were not very deep, how far would Tevbaugh have gone with the other false tunnel?

She stepped into the tunnel telling herself that she merely wanted to see if he had marked the way more fully or if he had only indicated the correct tunnel. Inside, she found that the shimmering line of blue continued along the wall of the tunnel, like the illuminated escape route in an office building or on an airplane. She chipped at the line with her fingernail trying to determine if it was a fluorescent mineral deposit or something more akin to chalk or paint. The line continued, unbroken, down the tunnel for a long distance until she reached a cul de sac. Justin had said that his tunnel ended in a rock fall, but this was a smoothly rounded room. Did the path continue somehow? Had she been mistaken about which tunnel each man had hone into?

Her hand found a thin crack in the wall that opened into a side tunnel. She squeezed through the little crack and emerged in another tunnel, blocked by a rockfall. The center was Hiram's initial tunnel then. She squeezed through the crack again, back to the cul de sac. Why had Tevbaugh directed her down a dead end? Had she missed something? She was suddenly angry with herself. It didn't matter! She needed to find a way to safety, away from Hiram and Justin, and possibly even Hoodoo. If she went back to the cave with the pool she could get down the mountain and try to find a way back to town. She turned and marched back toward the mouth of the tunnel dragging the fingers of her left hand along the shimmering line of fluorescent material wistfully. A noise in the main cavern stopped her short: voices.

"...has to be a trick..." she heard Hiram say.

She heard Justin's mumbled reply but could only make out "...rockfall..." She strained forward desperate to hear any other detail but could only make out the general mutter of conversation until Hiram's yell suddenly boomed through the tunnel.

"Check it again!" She had waited too long, and they were between her and the pool now, between her and escape. She needed to follow Tevbaugh's clues and get out. She turned back to the dead end and, moving as quietly as possible, tried to find some detail that she had missed before. She reached the cul de sac quickly, finding nothing.

"C'mon, c'mon," she whispered to herself, spinning on her heels in the tiny space. She stopped and took a breath. "If this was a geocache, what would I do?" She whispered, then in answer to herself said, "Look low, look high." She dropped to her knees and examined the sandstone wall where it met the floor. She held her makeshift water bottle lantern as close to the wall as she could but saw no glimmer of the fluorescent blue and no cut backs or ways to move under the stone.

"Okay, look high," she whispered and stood pushing the light as close to the ceiling as she could, only there was no ceiling there. She stared up in dawning realization: "The tunnel goes up." A tiny glimmer of blue caught her eye, just at the edge of the pool of light created by the glowing water bottle. She grumbled a small curse under her breath. She clicked on her headlamp so that she could better see her surroundings and saw, picked out by deep shadows, that there was a hand and toe trail up the wall: small divots that had been picked out of the soft material, just wide enough for her fingers and toes to connect with, like the handholds on a rock climbing wall. They went straight up. The water bottle had a small carabineer attached, which she clipped to her belt, then she tightened the straps on her pack and started climbing.

On a day when she was well rested and in good health, the climb would have been swift and easy with holds that were evenly spaced and obvious but, as it was, her already raw and shredded fingers protested at clinging to the gritty surface, and every reach sent a shock of electric pain across her ribs.

She stopped for a momentary rest when she was about eight feet above the floor of the cavern. A noise from below caught her attention and sent her heart into her throat. She reached up and clicked the headlamp off and realized that she could, once again, clearly see the shimmering line, the black light of the water bottle having been washed out by the bright white light of her headlamp. The line travelled straight up for a few more feet then spiraled to her left. She fumbled one-handed with the water bottle until it too went dark, but there was still light in the cavern below her. She pulled in a deep breath and held it. Justin stumbled into the room below her swinging his light wildly in a circle and kicking at random corners of the sandstone wall. Finally, he found the little crevice with its passage off to the tunnel he had explored on his first excursion, and he squeezed through. He never even looked up.

Mallory released the breath she had been holding and reached down to click on the sterilizer in the water bottle. The brilliant blue of the line she had been following sprang into life and she continued her climb. It was only a matter of time before Hoodoo or Hiram, who were both smarter than Justin, came to check this tunnel for themselves. They would almost certainly look up. She needed to get ahead of them.

The line of blue light, and the handholds, turned a bit more than 120 degrees, and she followed them like a spiral staircase. Soon, she came to an opening in the stone wall about the size of a window with an arrow etched just inside with the fluorescent material. She stepped sideways and into the opening.

A long, low tunnel extended off into the darkness and, even at her short stature, she found herself stooping to pass through it, her backpack scraping across the ceiling and leaving a shower of loose sandstone in her passing. Just as her neck started to ache from walking in a hunched posture the tunnel opened into a larger passage branching in four directions including both up and down. She tested each passage with the water bottle lamp until she found the one where the shimmering blue markings continued. Thankfully, it was one of the horizontal tunnels and not one of the vertical ones.

The tunnels branched and split over and over as she progressed, sometimes rising, sometimes falling. It was an enormous three-dimensional maze with some rooms and passages that appeared to be water worn, and others that showed tool marks on the walls that would indicate that Tevbaugh had either created the passage or widened it. Whatever this series of tunnels was, it must have honeycombed this whole section of the interior of the mesa. How had he discovered this passage? Or had he created it? Tevbaugh had acted both as Daedalus, building the Labyrinth of the Minotaur, and Ariadne providing a way for her lover to escape the maze. That would make her Theseus being led by the "thread" left in the labyrinth. Who or what then would be the monster in the maze, The Minotaur?

She decided after walking a bit more that Tevbaugh must have been a short man. The roof of the passage was frequently just above her head. If Hoodoo and Hiram had made it this far into the tunnel system, she imagined that they must be stooping quite a bit considering how much taller than her they were.

She lifted the water bottle lantern noticing that it was not as bright as before. Had she simply adjusted to the bizarre brilliance of the bulb, or were the batteries failing? As if in answer to her question, the bulb abruptly went out plunging her into blackness. She cursed and fumbled at her headlamp, trying to turn it on. There were other battery-operated things in the backpack, so she could swap out the power source. She began to slide the pack off but stopped.

There was a noise behind her, like voices from far away. She listened, frozen, but didn't hear it again. After a moment, she convinced herself that it was pareidolia: her brain attempting to make sense out of the tiny bit of sensory input it was receiving in the darkened passage. It had probably been an echo of her own pack straps slipping off her shoulders or a stone falling. Then, she heard it again. Somehow the men were catching up to her. How were they following her in the dark? She didn't have time to find the extra batteries. She'd have to sacrifice her headlamp. She ripped it off and popped open the back being careful not to drop the batteries that she knew she'd never find again in the dark.

Next was the purifier. She unscrewed the top of the device and pulled the batteries free noting their orientation within the device. She shoved the dead cells into her pocket and replaced the cap on the device clicking it on. It bloomed into light but wasn't as bright as a fresh set of batteries would be.

She listened behind her. The voices were louder now, a conversation in another room of a house. Why had she wondered about the Minotaur? Here they were!

She ran. Ahead of her the blue fluorescent line shimmered. How many times had she done this now? Run through some maze of Tevbaugh's with someone following? She wasn't even sure.

Ahead of her, the line took a sharp right turn and, as she followed it around the corner, she saw that it curved up the wall and ran for a short way on the ceiling before coming to an abrupt stop ending with a double arrow like two nested Vs. Was there another tunnel up? She skidded to a stop at the end of the line beneath the arrows, but there was no tunnel above her. The passage continued in a straight line with no side passages or breaks. The only difference she noticed was a slight downhill change in the grade. Had the line been removed somehow? Worn away? She began jogging down the passage, though more carefully than she had been, watching for other passages. The descent became steeper and soon she had picked up quite a bit of speed. Ahead of her, she thought she could see a glimmer of blue. She skidded to a stop sliding a few feet past her intended destination on the now steeply inclined ground.

She was shocked to feel open air beneath her extended leg. She carefully pulled back and held the makeshift lantern aloft. She was at the edge of a drop-off. She extended the lantern and saw a glimmering circle of blue that seemed to float in mid-air about five feet in front of her. The pool of light barely extended to it.

She stood carefully and braced herself in an effort to see what was ahead of her. She reached up to turn on the headlamp but remembered that it was no longer there. Cursing at her shortsightedness, she tried to push the lantern as far forward as she could. The circle of light resolved into the rim of a small round wooden platform. It was suspended from the roof of the passage by a length of rough hemp rope and dangled over the chasm that she had nearly skidded into. She knelt and extended the lantern into the darkness below, but the chasm was deep enough that the light was swallowed by darkness before reaching the bottom, if there was a bottom.

She could barely make out the other side of the chasm. Was she meant to leap the chasm with help of the small swinging platform? She reached out but could not snag the dangling rope. She wished once again for the geocaching bag that was in her own backpack knowing that there was a telescoping arm inside it that would extend her reach by three feet.

She thought she could make the leap, but she'd have to get a running start. Hopefully the rope wasn't rotten after hanging there for a hundred years. She turned and jogged back up the passage, which was made difficult by the incline. Ahead of her, she thought she could see the blue light of her water bottle lantern reflecting off the wall that marked the sharp turn in the tunnel. She was almost back to the double arrow marking on the ceiling. The light seemed darker, more purple than her own light, though. Were the batteries in her lantern about to go out again?

Suddenly, Hiram stepped around the corner. He was holding her own black light aloft. "Hey!" he bellowed, his deep voice filling the passage.

Mallory scrambled to a stop falling roughly on her hip and then flailed to regain her footing. She turned to run back the way she had come toward the chasm. She could hear the heavy footfalls of her pursuers, even over her own panting breaths, but they would be slower than her since they were bent nearly double to avoid the low ceiling.

She caught sight of the little floating platform and readied herself to jump, feeling a little twitch in her right thumb from the muscle memory of jumping Mario over millions of just such obstacles.

When the platform was as bright and clear as she thought it would ever be, she leapt, foot connecting with the platform, hand closing around the rough rope as it swung forward from her momentum, rope groaning from the weight, the loud creak of it filling the cavern. When she felt like it was at the zenith of its arc, she released the rope praying she had the momentum to carry herself over the gap.

There was a terrifying moment of weightlessness before gravity reasserted its hold on her, and she found herself crashing into stone floor. She skidded a bit in the loose sand but managed to stay mostly upright. It would never be a point winning dismount, but she was alive. The dangling platform jittered back and forth over the chasm in a shallow arc, losing its momentum.

She gathered herself together and looked around for Tevbaugh's marking, groaning inwardly when she spotted another double arrow above her head. Did that mean that there was another chasm ahead? Before she could get more than a few steps down the passage a booming voice cut the air.

"Mallory! Maaaaaaaalloreeeeeeeeeeee! Girl! I'm gonna catch you." It was Hiram; his whiskey and cigarettes voice scraped the tunnel walls leaving her feeling chilled. His words weren't a threat, just a cold statement of fact. She tried not to look behind to see where they were in the tunnel. They were coming, and that's all that mattered.

"Mallory girl!" he called again, reminding her of the way some people talked to dogs as if they owned them rather than the dog being their companions or friends. "That gold is mine, girl! I ain't never lettin' you off this mesa with it! Mark me, girl!"

She heard a thump and a loud grunt followed by rustling. Someone had made the leap over the chasm.

"Go! Go git her, boy!" Hiram bellowed. Justin had made the jump and would be coming down the tunnel.

She poured on what speed that she could muster keeping the lantern in front of her. Behind her she could hear the pounding of Justin's footfalls. In the distance, she saw a glimmer of blue and prepared to jump.

The edge of the chasm came into view, and the platform suspended there was clear. She leapt but felt her left ankle collide with the platform rather than landing on it as she had before. Her hand closed on the rope, and she swung forward with only her left hand to support her, feet kicking in air and

154

right hand flailing wildly. The ancient hemp dug into her palm reopening the rips in her hand. She released the rope earlier than she should with a scream of pain and found herself falling into the chasm rather than onto the stone floor. She desperately clutched with her right arm and managed to grab a large handhold that stuck up above the level of the floor. Her body slammed into the wall of the chasm, and all of her weight was leveraged onto her shoulder, wrenching it terribly and sending a lance of pain through her arm and shoulders, but she kept her grip. She dangled there for a moment; her entire weight on her fingertips, then swung her left arm up, and found purchase with it as well. Groaning with effort, she pulled herself up until her upper body was across the ledge with just her feet dangling into the pit.

She stayed like that for a moment relishing the solidity of the ground beneath her. From behind her came a soft chuckle and warm yellow light. Justin had caught up with her while all of her attention had been on preventing herself from falling into the darkness below.

"I don't even need to chase you. Looks like you're going to take yourself out before I get a chance to," he sneered at her. "Wait there, I'll come over and help you the rest of the way into that hole. Daddy wants to be the one to take you out, but you and me got beef. I still owe you for my knee."

She heard him backing up into the cavern as he spoke, giving himself the distance he'd need to run and jump to the other side. She rolled onto her side, pulling the rest of her weight onto the floor, and heard the nylon of the backpack rip. She shucked the straps from her shoulders; she'd need to be free of it if she had to fight Justin anyway.

The sound of his running alerted her, and her head snapped up. She saw him jump and, acting on impulse, her arm swung heaving the heavy pack in his direction, shoulder screaming protest. The pack connected with him in midair before he had even reached the still swinging platform. He and the pack swirled around each other and he became entangled with it, straps and rope flying loose, clothing and food packets falling from inside. Looking for all the world like he was clutching the pack to his chest, he fell straight down into the darkness.

CHAPTER FOURTEEN

"Justin!" Mallory screamed and dropped to the edge of the chasm. He had landed with a heavy thud and a muffled groan. The light of her water bottle lantern did not reach into the chasm enough to illuminate him, and only his moaning let her know that he was still alive. "Justin... can you talk?"

The scuffing sound of footsteps filled the cavern building from a whisper, and she knew that Hiram and Hoodoo would be there soon. Their stooped gait in the low roofed passage would slow them but not enough. She wasn't sure how they had managed to jump the chasm without running, but they clearly had figured something out.

"Justin, I'm sorry. You're dad's coming. He's coming. You'll be okay." She backed away from the chasm cradling her injured shoulder with her free hand. There were a few items that had fallen from the pack, and she gathered what she could and backed into the passage until the pool of light from her make-shift lantern was just at the edge of the chasm. She looked ahead into the tunnel and saw the beginning of the glowing blue line then clicked off the lantern and waited. It didn't take long for Hiram and Hoodoo to emerge from the passage.

"Stop!" She called firmly into the cavern backing in the passage a bit more so that their lights did not reach her.

"Where you at, girlie?" Sneered Hiram. "Where's my boy?"

"He fell. He's in the chasm. I think he's hurt."

There was a moan from the chasm that might have been Justin trying to speak.

"You know. I was gonna let you go girl. I was really just trying to keep you off the mesa. But this... you stepped in it now." His cold voice was a thin veneer over a rage that she could feel across the darkened room.

"I just wanted..." she started.

"Run," he said quietly.

"I just..." she tried again.

"RUN!" he bellowed at her and swung the rifle that had been dangling in his hand up to his shoulder firing a shot before it even settled into place. The noise assaulted her in the small space echoing again and again down the tunnel. A spray of sandstone chips bounced off of her shoulder.

"Hiram!" Hoodoo yelled and slammed his shoulder into the man. Hiram pitched forward firing again as he came down hard on a knee. The second shot blasted a hole into the ceiling of the tunnel just above Mallory's head. Hiram swung wildly with the butt of the rifle aiming for Hoodoo but missing by a wide margin. Hoodoo came up from a crouch and caught him under the arm mid swing. Both men skidded landing in a heap at the edge of the chasm.

"Go, Mallory! Run!" Hoodoo yelled at her from the tangle of limbs, but she remained frozen, fear gripping her. Hiram kicked ferociously at Hoodoo and sent him into a sprawl, head and shoulders hanging over the pit, a smear of blood across his nose, black in the purple glow of the blacklight. Hiram pulled himself to his feet and placed his booted foot between Hoodoo's shoulders then brought the rifle up again.

"Yeah, girl," he growled, "you'd better run."

Mallory ran.

* * *

The sleek red and white helicopter settled onto the desert floor and discharged two men in fluorescent yellow jackets who jogged to the Jeep where Deputy Reyes and Lynn stood, shielding their eyes from the sand and grit that the chopper churned into the air.

"Deputy Reyes?" the first man said loudly trying to be heard over the steady thumping of the chopper blades. Reyes extended his hand with a sharp nod. "Dixon Carver," he said, introducing himself, then indicated the other man, "Jeff Koval. What do we have? Lost hikers?"

"Uh... a bit more than that," Reyes brought them up to speed as quickly as he could giving them the coordinates of the last point of contact and explaining about the gunshots and their suspicions about Hiram.

"Are there injuries?" Koval asked, pulling off his helmet and shaking free a head of unruly curls.

"Unknown," said Reyes, "but I won't rule it out."

"Do you suppose they've travelled east or west of last contact?" Carver asked.

"My guess would be towards the main body of the mesa," Lynn answered.

"I'm sorry," Carver said, seeming to notice her for the first time, "who are you in this?"

"Lynn Estes, I'll be your guide..." she began.

"We don't need a guide from the air--" Carver started but Reyes cleared his throat and stepped forward leaning in until he was right by Carver's ear.

"You won't get off the ground without her," he whispered. "Let's just save the time, get in the chopper, and get started. Besides, she knows the area better than anyone here."

Carver leaned to the side until he was looking at Lynn over Reyes' shoulder. For her part, Lynn simply crossed her arms and tightened her jaw muscle. When he still seemed unconvinced she narrowed her eyes and glared at him.

"Yeah. Okay. People in trouble," he said with a false joviality. "At your last contact they were on top of the mesa, correct? Not on the ground between the formations?"

"You took your sweet time getting here so that was 10 hours ago. They could be anywhere at this point," Lynn said.

"And if they're trying to avoid Hiram they may not be moving in any particular pattern," Reyes tossed in, trying to defuse the insult that Lynn had just lobbed into the mix.

"Right," Carver said, his eyes still firmly on Lynn, voice hard. "Okay, then it's probably best to concentrate on the quadrant between last contact and the mesa, defaulting to the desert side of the formations. They might be trying to find a way out," Carver started toward the helicopter. "This way. We'll get you suited up, helmets and harnesses, and get into the air. Even with a limited search area this might take a while."

As Carver and Koval started toward the helicopter, Lynn lightly knocked Reyes in the chest with the back of her hand. "Hey. Thanks."

"Just trying to get Carey out of this mess he got himself into as quick as I can," Reyes said.

"Like I said. Thanks."

* * *

The tunnel had not deviated for an eternity. After the two chasms with their rope platforms, there had been a few turns with choices of tunnel and one climb down into a pit, but since then Mallory had been walking in a straight line through an uninterrupted and unchanged chute. There were no signs that Hiram, Justin or Hoodoo had left the chasm to pursue her. She was alone, and the feeling that she was buried alive in this mountain was beginning to crush her from all directions.

Her water bottle lantern flickered went out, and she cursed. It was the second time that it had gone dark. The first time she was plunged into darkness she had panicked and nearly hyperventilated. She had fumbled with the batteries she had in her pocket, swapping them in and out of the water purification device until she found a combo that had enough juice to return her to light. The relief left her weeping and shaking.

The light of the lantern had been weak, and she had known it wouldn't last very long. She took inventory of the few items that she had grabbed before she ran and found that she was carrying a first aid and survival kit, a packet of freeze dried apple crumble, a freezer bag full of instant coffee, another bag that contained a toothbrush and a travel sized toothpaste, and the little leather notebook that had belonged to Hoodoo's dad.

There were no fresh batteries in the commercially assembled survival pack, but there were two glow sticks. Without the ultraviolet light of the water bottle, she was lost but, at least, she wasn't in the dark. She scrubbed away the tear that welled to her eye and opened the survival kit to find the glow stick.

An image of her parents floated into her mind in the darkness. Her mom would probably spend Mallory's funeral shoving foil covered casserole dishes into the oven and bustling around the house taking care of Mallory's friends and other relatives. It was just what her mom did. Her dad would probably spend most of it in the garage sipping on the bottle of whisky that he had hidden above his work bench in open defiance of her mother, even though Mallory knew that her mother was fully aware of it, letting him have his 'secret' stash so that he felt like he was getting away with something. Her brother would probably do the same thing he did on most days: play video games.

What would the headline of her obituary read? Would her death make news beyond the obits? "Promising UNC student found dead in the Utah desert." She thought that headline would be good, but more probably it would read, "Disgraced UNC student."

Her fingers finally found the glow stick, and she snapped it and shook it then slumped against the wall to wait for the light to blossom from it.

There was the real problem. If she died out here, then Jonathan Toller was going to get away with it. He'd bury the evidence of her find, and he'd be the toast of the archaeological world based on lies and falsehood. She was the only person who had any proof of what had happened.

She pulled in a shuddering breath. With no ability to follow Tevbaugh's path, she was lost. Who knew that the Minotaur in this maze would turn out not to be Hiram after all, but the Energizer Bunny. When she was satisfied that the glow stick was as bright as it ever would be, she dusted herself off and resumed her march down the seemingly endless tunnel. Ahead of her, she could see that something changed. The walls came to an end, and there were no rock surfaces bouncing the light back to her beyond that. It looked like she was walking into nothingness. Even as she drew closer, that feeling didn't change. No walls, no floor, just a massive hole in reality.

When she reached the end of the tunnel, she started to understand. The floor dropped away from the end of the tunnel sharply before leveling out. The walls and ceilings opened up into an inverted bowl so that she was in a large, circular room with a domed ceiling. It was about fifty feet across and probably twenty feet high at the center of the dome. The weak light of the glow stick barely reached the ceiling, but she could see that it was covered in marks and lines in a chaotic dance of shape, light and darkness.

She dug into the survival kit and pulled out the second glow stick, cracking it and doubling the light in the room. Above her, in the surreal watery light of the chemical glow sticks, were thousands, perhaps hundreds of thousands, of petroglyphs. It was a Native American Sistine Chapel with markings large and small. Layer upon layer of marks chipped out of the thin magnesium coating that covered the walls revealing the lighter colored sandstone beneath. It was an undisturbed masterpiece of Native American art bigger than any single collection of petroglyphs that she knew of in the United States, possibly the world. Here were animals, people, and gods, telling the stories of tribes and nations to anyone who knew how to read them. It would be a lifetime's work for an archaeologist; a career could be made of this. Perhaps her career, if she ever made it out.

She walked around the rim of the room in awe at the massive scope of the work. Was it created by a single person? A tribe of people? After several yards, she noticed a strong straight line that run up from the floor perpendicularly. She followed it to the center of the room and found herself standing underneath a massive petroglyph. It had a dozen lines radiating from it in the same manner to all corners of the room.

She stared at the petroglyph in awe feeling that it was familiar somehow. She dug into her pocket, pulled out her shattered phone, and brought the screen to life. She scrolled through the pictures until she found the three goddess petroglyphs from the Frenchman's map. She had identified Mary and Bast, and now the third petroglyph was there above her head. It had multiple arms and sat in the center of a spoked wheel of lines like a spider web. Did this represent 'Grandmother Spider' or the 'Old Spider Woman?' She knew that the Hopi, Zuni, and Pueblo had a tradition of that figure in their mythology. Did it extend to this area as well? She wasn't sure.

She followed one of the radiating lines across the ceiling to the floor and realized that there was a small cavity where the wall met the floor: a low tunnel. She ran around the circumference of the room checking and realized that there were tunnels at the end of each of the radiating spokes. One of these was probably her way out of the room. She had no doubt that if her lantern were working she would see a blazing line of blue fluorescent paint pointing directly at one of them. Without it she had a one in twelve shot of choosing the correct tunnel. She could take her chances and choose at random, or she could lay in wait, allow the men to catch up, and hope that their black light was still in working order. Neither seemed like a good plan.

She returned to the tunnel she had emerged from and began a systematic search crawling a few feet in and checking for anything unusual. By the time she had completed a circuit around the room, she had been able to eliminate the tunnels at 3, 4 and 8 o'clock, all of which had been blocked after just a few feet. Her second time around yielded nothing but frustration. Time passed, and her glows sticks grew weaker. If the men had gotten across the last chasm, they could emerge from the tunnel at any minute.

She tried again to search the tunnels. At each one, she grew more despondent. There were no changes. No signs of variation or markings or direction. She dropped to her hands and knees holding the glow sticks between her teeth and crawled forward into the tunnel at 7 o'clock. Her palms ached, her shoulder screamed each time she moved forward, and the bruise on her ribs sent lances of pain through her if she stretched too far with each move. She was a bundle of aches and crawling around in the tunnel was adding her knees and back to the list. The tunnel seemed to be just like all the others, and the fruitlessness of it was starting to weigh on her. She decided to extend the distance she had crawled into each of the previous tunnels hoping that if she went just a little farther she might find something.

Her mind went back to her parents. Her brother would have told them by now. There was no way he could have waited the full 72 hours she had asked for. Her mom had total control over him. The headline of her obituary floated into her mind again. Maybe that headline would never say that she was found dead; here, buried under the mesa, it would probably just read "Missing UNC Student Declared Dead, Body Never Recovered."

She shrieked pulling her hand back and slamming her shoulders into the roof of the tunnel. She had touched something furry! She started to back out but stopped. There, on the floor of the tunnel where the glow sticks had fallen out of her mouth, was a mouse. It stood on its haunches and squeaked in defiant indignation then bounded down the tunnel away from her.

"Wait!" she called, and started after it stopping only to collect her glow sticks. "Where are you going? I haven't seen so much as a fly in these tunnels, but here you are! Do you know the way out?" She crawled after it desperately dragging her few meager belongings along with her. She didn't have much, and she certainly wasn't going to give up anything that she had. A few dozen feet down the tunnel she saw some leaves. She had lost the mouse, but the leaves stood as confirmation that the tunnel connected to the outside world in some way. In another dozen feet, she started seeing light. The floor was littered with rotting leaves and debris that she crunched through happily; her heart suddenly filled with joy at the prospect of being out from under the rock of the mesa.

At the end of the tunnel, she found a small pool of dark water stained with rotting leaves and other organic matter, but a cascade of light fell onto the pool from above. She stood, the pool lapping just at her ankles, and exulted at the feeling of standing straight again. Above her was a tangle of roots and vines; she had emerged beneath the root ball of a tree. Had this been the path that Tevbaugh intended her to take? She wasn't sure. Maybe in the century since he had been there, the tree and water had found their way into one of his dead ends. She didn't care. There was light and freedom above her. She just needed to hack her way through.

She pulled and tugged at the roots maneuvering through the openings that she created and pushing with her legs to leverage herself through. Roots bent and snapped below her, but she pulled and struggled keeping herself upright. Finally, her hand jutted through the tangled mass, and she emerged, inch by inch, from the grave she had been in. She was free of the tunnels, reborn into a world of light.

She fell onto her back in a tuft of grass and relished the view of the sky above her. Looking around, she realized where she had emerged: at the bottom the Frenchman's Eye. It seemed like years ago that Hoodoo had described the formation to her calling it a "hole." It was so much more than that.

She was at the bottom of a large cylindrical formation, like being at the bottom of a soup can. The spring that had probably eroded the formation into the mesa fell in a sparkling strand from the tall wall opposite her. At the bottom, it splashed into a pool out of which flowed a tiny stream. The stream meandered across the floor terminating in another pool. She assumed that it sunk into the mesa there, possibly providing the source of water she had drunk from back in Bast's cave.

All around her was a riparian paradise created by the water. There were tall cottonwoods that reached majestically for the sky above them, and she could hear birds and the buzzing of insects. The whole thing was a terrarium-like oasis of life. It was no wonder that this place was called "Paradise."

Then her heart sank. She was once again trapped. The walls soared all around her, and Hoodoo had told her that the only way anyone had found to the bottom had been repelling. She had no equipment, and there was no way she had the strength, stamina or experience to free climb the 300 feet to the top. She had emerged from one grave into a completely different type of grave, but a grave nonetheless. She blinked back a tear and started walking.

She followed the line of the stream towards the welcoming sound of the tiny waterfall stumbling over stones and logs as she progressed. If she couldn't escape, she'd need somewhere to hide. She had cornered herself and, if Hiram found his way out of the maze, there was no longer any room to run.

A strange sight came into view: a small rustic cabin. The walls were rough-hewn timber that was barely different from fallen trees. The walls slumped sideways in an oddly drunken parody of a house. One wall featured a crude mud and stone chimney, partially collapsed. She looked around. The cabin was slightly raised above the ground and appeared to be built on a hill or outcropping. It was almost central to the area of the Frenchman's Eye, and there were windows, at least on the two sides that she could see. It could be the best option for a place to hide and watch for Hiram and Hoodoo to emerge. If the tunnel that she had taken had not actually been the one Tevbaugh had intended, they may come out in a different spot, and she'd need to be able to see all around her to keep watch.

The tiny cabin wasn't much larger than a bathroom in a modern house. She pulled at the door, and it fell from its hinges with a crash, flopping onto the side of the cabin. Inside was not in great shape either with missing floorboards and pinholes of light pouring through the walls and ceilings. She imagined many treasure hunters had picked over the little house. In one corner was a rusted iron bed frame that still held a few scraps of rotted ticking; a pile of straw and cotton that stood in a drift in the corner was all that was left of whatever mattress had been on it. The collapsed carcass of a potbelly stove slumped on one side of the room having rusted past the point of holding itself together. Most of the window glass was long ago broken away. The cabin was barely standing, but it provided for her immediate need: a place to hide and get herself together.

She took stock of herself and suddenly felt gross. Her clothes were filthy, covered in a dark grime, not to mention blood, and probably every other form of filth. Her hands, and the bandanas still tied across her palms, were black with layer of grime that extended past her elbows in a gritty coating. Her pants were likewise dark with the dirt and dust. She looked like she had been playing a fire pit. Maybe she could clean herself up in the tiny stream.

Her stomach complained, reminding her of how long it had been since she'd eaten. She ripped open the foil packet of freeze dried apple crumble and sniffed at it. It smelled okay even if it looked like instant oatmeal. She poured in a little of her water to rehydrate it and set it aside. She wished she had a way of heating it considering that it was the last food she had. Possibly the last food she'd ever have since she was at the bottom of a pit, even if it was a beautiful pit, with no way to contact the outside world and no way out except back through a pitch black maze with no light.

While her lunch rehydrated, she went to the stream. Ahead, at the edge of the streambed, there was a spot of brilliant white beneath a layer of fallen leaves. She headed toward it, listening to the lazy burble of the stream. The closer she got to it, the more out of place it seemed: pure white in the organic surroundings. She turned to it. With her limited supplies, anything manufactured could be useful, and treasure hunters could have abandoned anything down here. When she reached it and smoothed back the leaves, she found the last thing she ever would have expected: a drone. She carefully pulled away the leaves and twigs that had accumulated on top of it. Hadn't Hoodoo mentioned a treasure hunter piloting a drone down here looking for the Frenchman's treasure? She thought it was even one of the models that she had worked with back on the dig in Arizona. It appeared to be mostly in good shape, all of the rotors were intact. She flipped it over shaking her head at the irony of that. There was a nasty crack across the bottom, the battery door was missing, leaving the compartment open. The battery had fallen out. She kicked a few of the leaves until she spotted the bright blue rectangle of the battery and picked it up as well. It felt strange, not like the smooth batteries she had used on the dig, and the wrapping was puffy. She'd bring it to the cabin she decided; perhaps it had some component that she might be able to salvage.

Her hands refused to come clean. With no soap, the best she could hope for was removing the upper layer of filth. It would have to be enough. She returned to the cabin and checked on the rehydrating food. She grimaced at the cold mush. It would never be palatable. She shuffled through the other things she had and used the toothbrush to stir the mush around and tasted it from the end of the handle. It wasn't the worst thing she'd ever eaten, but it was never going to satisfy her desire for real food.

As she ate, she considered her situation while pacing around the small cabin in an attempt to keep watch in all possible directions. Eventually, she slowed and stopped, sitting on the frame of one of the windows. If Hiram and Hoodoo came out of the maze, would Hiram kill her right away? What if Justin was alive and with them? Would his injuries slow them down? Hoodoo had stepped between her and Hiram at least twice now, both times taking injuries of his own. As she thought, her thumbnail picked at a lump in the wooden window frame absently. Would Hiram even let Hoodoo leave the maze, or would he kill Hoodoo as well? She knew so little about the man that she couldn't begin to predict how he'd react to anything.

Outside there was a rush of noise, and she stepped quickly to the opposite window. A flock of small birds rose from the dry branches of a nearby tree and ascended towards the sky. She scanned but couldn't see anything that would have disturbed them.

167

"Take me with you!" she muttered and resumed her pacing around the circumference of the room pausing at each window to be sure that the men emerging from the depths of the mountain hadn't been the thing that disturbed the birds.

Across the cabin, a small glint of light caught her eye, and she looked back at the window. Something on the frame glittered in the sunlight. She bent to examine it and realized that it was the lump she had been worrying with her thumbnail. There, beneath the grime and corrosion, was the head of a nail. It appeared to be made of gold.

CHAPTER FIFTEEN

Mallory bent and stared at the nail head. It was about a quarter of an inch square, deep brown with age and patina. In the center of the nail head was a mark, but she couldn't quite make out what it was. She grabbed the toothpaste from her meager belongings and the toothbrush from beside her abandoned meal. She put a small dollop of the paste onto the brush and scrubbed at the nail for a few seconds until it gleamed. With her thumb, she wiped away the toothpaste. She was sure of it now. Here was a golden nail head, and there in the center of it was the petroglyph of the deer from the map etched into the head.

She slowly examined the circumference of the window looking for other nails or marks, but found nothing. She moved to the next window. She methodically moved around the frame inspecting it with both eyes and fingertips. She found two nails in the sill, but they both appeared to be regular iron nails. She continued up the side of the frame and found another nail. She scraped at the brown surface with her fingernail, and a small flake of brown patina came away revealing gold beneath. Her breath caught. She scrubbed at the nail with the toothbrush, bringing it up to a high polish then leaned in to inspect it. In the head was the glyph of a house.

"Tevbaugh! You clever old coot!" she called out. "What is this? What have you done?" Her heart racing, she continued around each window, then the doorframe. She only found one other nail. She grabbed the notebook and flipped to the page that bore the list of glyphs that appeared on the map. There was the deer and the house and the dagger that she had found on a nail in the doorframe, along with 11 other glyphs. How long would it take her to find all of the nails? She fell to her knees and started in one corner of the cabin following a row of floorboards to the opposite wall. Almost immediately, she found a nail bearing the glyph of a ladder. She rummaged in the survival kit and extracted a spool of medical tape. She ripped off small squares and marked all the nails that she had found so far. Even if she found all thirteen glyphs, it wouldn't help if she had to search for them a second time.

As she slid her hands across the rough planks of the floor, a thought occurred to her: the treasure, if it existed, had been hidden for more than a century despite hundreds of people looking for it. If the clues for the final goddess were here, that most likely meant that the treasure was here as well. A hiding place that could keep a secret from hundreds of determined searchers would probably keep *her* safe from Hiram. She picked up the pace.

When she found the fifth, she realized that the nails were all slightly raised from the board they were in, just enough to feel. She marked it with tape and felt across the floor for more. It took her 20 minutes to examine the entire floor, and she found three other nails, the final one beneath the pile of rust and deteriorated metal that used to be the stove. She had seven of the thirteen glyphs.

Next were the walls. She found them more difficult to examine, but she concentrated first on the upright beams that supported the external walls. Half an hour later, she had four more nails. There were thirteen glyphs that formed the trail, and she had found twelve nails. Would they all match? Would there be more?

She dropped into a seated position on the floor and pulled the notebook to her double-checking the list; she was missing the heart, the starting point. She looked at the image of the final goddess from the map on her phone. Tevbaugh had said, "Weave as the spider." She wasn't sure what that meant. She flipped through the notebook to the very beginning looking for a list of the items Tevbaugh had supposedly had with him when he died. So far, they had proven to be the keys to the mystery. She found it on the third page: a rosary, a quartz crystal attached to a tin plate, and a spool of twine. She glanced around the room at the constellation of white dots that marked the nail heads. How did twine help with this? She could weave with twine. Did weaving 'as the spider' mean a web?

The survival kit didn't have twine... what could she weave with? Her eyes landed on the spool of medical tape. There wasn't much, but perhaps there would be enough if she split the tape in the center. She snipped the tape with some small scissors that were in the first aid kit and started spooling the tape out. If the pattern followed the pattern of symbols on the map, she would start with the heart, but she hadn't found that yet. Instead, she'd need to start with the deer, the second symbol. She tacked the tape to the nail that bore the symbol of the deer and stretched it to the wall across the cabin and the ladder-marked nail. She continued in that fashion following to the house, the dagger, cactus, feather, the teepee, the turtle, campfire, bow, cloud, and finally to the sign of the mesa and stepped back. A series of brilliant white slashes cut through the space crossing the room repeatedly from side to side.

"I don't get it Tevbaugh," she said. "What am I supposed to be seeing here?"

She stepped into the room ducking between lengths of tape. There was one place in the room where the tape crossed itself: the floor.

"Does 'X' mark the spot?" she mused aloud and maneuvered until she was standing on the cross. She slowly turned in a circle looking at the shapes formed by the tape. A length of tape just skimmed the top of her head. Was that meant to be eye level? She knew from the way the tunnel had been dug through the mesa that she and Tevbaugh were of a similar height. She hoped that if what she was meant to see was dependent on angle, as the sighting of the granary through the arches had been, that she was close enough to his height for it to work.

When she had turned completely around, she sighed. "Maybe 'X' doesn't mark the spot after all. Is it the heart? Would the heart make sense of this?" She rocked her head back in a thinking pose staring up at the ceiling. A large log cut through the center of the space acting as a rafter or beam of some sort. A large daddy longlegs crawled lazily across the beam. "Well, hello there Anansi," she said, "or is that you Grandmother Spider?"

She stretched up immediately dropping her right hand when her shoulder screamed in pain, but she couldn't quite reach the beam. She looked about and spotted a length of wood, a limb about a foot long that could have been part of a walking stick. She ducked out of the web of tape and picked it up. With the additional length, she could tap the beam, and she ran the stick along it feeling for the raised head of a nail. About a third of the way down the beam, the stick caught on something. She strained on her tiptoes to see it but couldn't make out whether it was another nail or just something sticking out of the log naturally.

There was nothing in the room to stand on to add to her height, so she'd have to jump. She pulled out a little length of tape and prepped it and then jumped toward what she hoped was a nail. It was awkward to do it with her left hand, and it took her three painful attempts, but eventually she stuck the tape fairly close to the 'nail.' She pulled out the length of tape and attached it to the nail marked with the deer, then returned to the center of the web.

She slowly turned on the 'X' again, heart sinking when there was still nothing. Three quarters of the way through her turn, she stopped dead. The lines in space coalesced suddenly and there, hanging in the air in front of her, was a gigantic arrow, pointing through one of the windows. She focused beyond the tip of the arrow at the wall of stone that surrounded her. There, at the point of the arrow, was a dark band of sandstone that crossed the undulating wall with a bold slash. Was that it? What that what she was meant to see?

"Huh," she said and took a step back moving her head back and forth to see if any other detail caught her attention. There was nothing. She looked up at the ceiling to see if the spider was still on the beam. "Anansi?" she said softly.

"Who the hell's Nancy?" came Hiram's voice from behind her. She spun to find the man framed in the doorway. He was filthy, mud-streaked and wet with sweat. The rifle was across his shoulder, and one arm was propped up on the butt. His mean eyes glared at her from the shadow cast by his hat. Some distance behind him she saw Hoodoo struggling to carry a limp but alive Justin. One of Justin's arms was over Hoodoo's shoulder, the other in a sling pulled tightly to his body. They both limped along. It was unclear which of them was helping and which was being helped.

"What'd you find?" Hiram demanded. "You know where my treasure is?" Mallory instinctively shrank back from him feeling the tape stick to her hair and pull free from the wall. It fluttered loosely draping over one of the other pieces. Hiram stepped up into the cabin. "I asked you a question, girly. What is all this mess?"

Hiram closed the distance between them in one big step. She tried to step back but ended up tangled in the tape. Hiram put his clawed hand on her shoulder, and she could smell the cigarettes and stale whisky on him as he leaned in close and gutturally whispered in her ear, "Where's the treasure, girly?"

His hand clamped onto her shoulder, thumb digging into the muscles that she had wrenched earlier, and she shrieked, going immediately to her knees, sobbing.

"Mallory!" She heard Hoodoo call, not far away now.

"I'll show you," she said between wracking breaths.

"Good girl," Hiram brayed, "maybe I'll let you live after all." He grabbed a handful of her hair and yanked her to her feet shoving her toward the door in one vicious movement. She stumbled, and Hoodoo caught her. He had a black eye, and his moustache and beard were caked with blood. There were two lengths of climbing rope clipped to his belt loops at either side. All together it all made him look like a zombie rock climber.

"Mallory!" He whispered, "Are you hurt?"

She shook her head curtly. Behind him she could see Justin propped against a tree cradling his bandaged arm. Her backpack was beneath one of his ankles elevating his leg.

"He's in a bad way," Hoodoo said, following her line of sight. "Arm's probably broken, and I think he hit his head. He hasn't said a lot, keeps drifting away."

She drew her wrist across her face scrubbing away a tear. "Let's get this over with," she growled at whoever was listening and stomped off toward the dark spot in the rock that had been at the point of the arrow not caring if either of the men followed her.

"Quite the firecracker you found, Carey," Hiram said in gravelly drawl. "She might be able to do what your daddy never could."

"Don't talk about my daddy," Hoodoo said in a low growl emphasizing each word.

Hiram snorted, "Still a little boy, believe your daddy's Superman and can do anything." Mallory thought she could hear Hoodoo take a deep breath and hold it for a few heartbeats before releasing it.

They crossed the distance in relative silence. There was nothing but the sound of their boots in sand and rock, and birdsong. If they hadn't all been streaked with sweat, filth and blood, they could be a group of friends on a hike.

As they drew closer to the wall, Mallory started to see that the rippling wall of stone ahead of them had deep depressions and grooves cut into it and below a few of them were a talus of stones. Were these mine tailings, the rocks and stones removed from a mineshaft as it dug deeper into the earth? Had Tevbaugh mined something here rather than hiding something?

She slowly cast her eyes to either side wondering if there was a better choice than simply leading Hiram to the treasure. Was there another place to hide? Another place to run? Hiram had been herding them since the first gunshot, and he was counting on his physical superiority and her own fear to drive her now. It was the same thing Toller had done minus the gun. They had both bullied her into a position where she had no choice but to allow them to make the decisions and receive the glory because she was too meek to speak up for herself. Well, it was time to put a stop to that.

"Hey, Hoodoo!" she called back over her shoulder, "Are you with this redneck idiot or not?"

"Ha!" Hiram guffawed. "This daddy's boy is with whatever I say he's with. Keep walking, girly."

"That right, Hoodoo?" she asked, pointedly not looking back at them. Twenty heartbeats passed. Had she misread what was going on?

"I'm with you, Mal," she finally heard him say. "Always was."

"What are you on about boy?" she heard Hiram say, and his loping steps stopped abruptly. "You owe me!"

She kept walking but heard Hoodoo's steps stop as well.

"I don't owe you squat! I listened to you bad mouth my daddy all my life, and I'm done!"

"I took you in when that piece of trash found himself dead at the bottom of a cliff," Hiram bellowed. Mallory turned, the two men were face to face now, and Hiram seemed to have forgotten her. His face was red with rage, and he was gripping the stock of the gun so fiercely that she thought he might crack it.

"You took me in so you could claim Daddy's life insurance," Hoodoo said coldly, and she saw his own hand close around the barrel of the rifle.

"I treated you right!"

"You treated me like a mule you could work every waking hour and then beat me whenever you felt like it!"

Mallory slammed into Hiram.

She'd had enough distance between them to get a good momentum, and her smaller stature allowed her to bring her shoulder into his abdomen just below his ribs. She drove up at the last moment knocking his breath out of him and throwing him backwards. Hiram pitched to his side with a loud grunt, landing hard, but he managed to keep a grip on the rifle pulling Hoodoo forward in a tangle of limbs. The two men scuffled, each trying to pull the gun away from the other. Unsure what else she could do, Mallory kicked Hiram. Her boot connected with his shoulder blade, sending a shockwave up her own leg but not seeming to affect Hiram at all. She brought her boot down again, this time eliciting a growl from him.

On her third kick, Hiram released the stock of the gun, and his hand shot out like a snake, closing around her ankle. He yanked viciously throwing her onto Hoodoo with a ferocious strength. She yelped with surprise and tried to roll backwards off the man. Hoodoo pushed at her, rolling onto his back.

The loud KA-KLACK of a rifle bolt stopped them both. Mallory looked up at the barrel of the rifle that Hiram had retrieved and now had trained on her head.

"Get up!" he snarled at them, "I didn't want to kill you Carey, but you ain't making that easy." He dug the sharp toe of his cowboy boot into Hoodoo's rib. "Get. UP!" he bellowed.

Mallory managed to get to her feet first and helped Hoodoo onto his. He winced when he put weight onto his leg but shook his head when she tried to ask about it.

"Now. Where's the treasure, girl?"

Mallory slowly lifted her arm, pointing at the dark band of material embedded in the sandstone. "There," she said quietly.

"Doesn't look like much," Hiram retorted, "but let's see. Move!"

Mallory and Hoodoo started walking.

"I'm sorry... I couldn't..." Hoodoo started in a whisper.

Mallory stopped him. "Shhh. We'll figure it out."

"It was the only way I thought I could..."

"Shhh," she said. "One right thing. Just find the one right thing."

When they reached the wall, there was a small scramble over the loose rock. Just below the dark band there was a thick bulge of sandstone that curved away from the wall. There was a clear mass of loose stone at one side of the bulge.

Hiram extended the gun between Mallory and Hoodoo, pressing it against Mallory's chest, and bringing her to a stop. "Check it out," he demanded. "She'll keep me company out here."

Hoodoo met Mallory's eyes with an apology. "It's okay," she said. "Check it out."

He went to the side of the bulge, loose stone skidding beneath his feet and clattering down the small mound. Mallory watched him put his hand on the bulge, sliding it toward the wall, following the undulations and ripples in the stone.

"I don't..." he started, then said, "Oh," and took a step sideways, disappearing.

Hiram stepped to the side, pushing Mallory with his shoulder. "Where?" he said.

Hoodoo's awed voice called from somewhere behind the stone wall, "Holy!"

"What, boy! What is it?" Hiram called and stepped forward.

"I've never seen anything like it, Uncle Hiram! I've never..." Hoodoo's voice trailed off. Hiram stalked forward forgetting about Mallory, the gun hanging loosely from his hand. He reached up, imitating Hoodoo's movements seeking the entrance to wherever he had disappeared to.

Mallory leapt forward with a guttural inhuman snarl crashing into Hiram's back with all the weight and force she could muster, pitching him forward into the stone. His face smashed into the sandstone wall, and he recoiled, leaving a smear of blood on the wall and a matching one across his nose and cheek. He spun, growling like a bear, gun raised like a club to hit her.

"You little..." he growled.

Mallory ducked and lunged to his side. Hiram spun in place, trying to follow her motions but the loose scree slid away underneath him, scattered by his sudden movement. He went down, with his legs splayed, sliding in the loose stone. At the last minute, he lashed out with the butt of the gun, still using it like a club, and connected with her hip, sending her to the ground beside him. They both slid down the rock face. Mallory caught herself first and scrambled upward again, sending a clatter of stone down onto his shoulders. He responded with an angry growl.

"Get back here, girl,' he said, and regained his feet.

"Carey!" she screamed, as he stepped out of the rock crevice. Hoodoo leapt past her and caught Hiram in a flying bear hug. Hiram's feet skidded in the rock, and he fell backward with Hoodoo's momentum. The two men landed with a loud combined grunt. Hiram's gun clattered past them.

Hoodoo pushed himself up, towering over the prostrate Hiram. "Get up!" he yelled, fist already cocked to the side, "GET UP!"

Hiram groaned, shifting slightly. Mallory came to Hoodoo's side and placed a hand on his outstretched fist, "I don't think he can. He's down." Hoodoo remained in that position, fist cocked and ready to loose, until his shoulder shook with the tension of it. When it was clear that Hiram was not going to move again he lowered his arm and released a shuddering breath. Mallory quietly reached over and unclipped one of the spools of climbing rope from his belt and put it into his hand. "Tie him up. He can't hurt us anymore."

The two worked together, securing Hiram's arms and legs. Hoodoo's fingers pulled the rope into quick knots, and he ripped a handkerchief from Hiram's own pocket and gagged him with it. Together, they repositioned him at the bottom of the rock slope. Hoodoo retrieved the rifle, and emptied it of ammunition. "Are you okay?" he asked her.

"Yeah," she said, breathlessly, "yeah."

"What are we going to do with them?" she asked. "How do we get out of here?"

"I don't know," he said honestly. "Your pack is back by the cabin. Is that rescue thing Lynn gave you still in it?"

"I used that yesterday," she said, "if it worked…"

"If it worked, then she's probably already out here, somewhere," he said, standing and dusting the grit and sand from his chest.

"Hoodoo…" she started, "I know this might not be the right time, but… what's in there? What is the treasure?"

He looked at her, lips curling into a wistful smile. "Nothing. It's just a little cave."

"Nothing?" She was crestfallen. All of this had been for nothing?

"C'mon," he said. I'll show you. They made their way back to the top of the scree, and he ducked his head from side-to-side until he spotted what he was looking for. He stepped back and extended his arm into a crack in the sandstone. It was scarcely wide enough for his chest, and from any other angle would have been practically invisible. He stepped through and disappeared. He poked his head and shoulders back out. "I've been down here a dozen times and never noticed it. I really thought I'd explored every square inch of this place." Hiram grunted and kicked his legs a little. "Guess you never found it either, Old Man," Hoodoo teased. He stepped back into the cave.

Mallory cast a sidelong glance at Hiram glaring at her from his position at the bottom of the rock pile then turned and shimmied through the small opening.

Inside, there was a thin shaft of light from the crack that provided a feeble glow in the room. Mallory found Hoodoo standing in a small circular space that had a large egg shaped boulder in the center. The boulder was taller than Hoodoo, almost as wide as it was tall. There was a narrow space all around it providing just enough room for a person to pass between the boulder and the wall. The shaft of daylight fell on boulder like a crack in the giant egg shape.

"See?" Hoodoo said, "Nothing. But Hiram's so desperate to find the treasure that he'd believe anything."

"Do you really think he killed your dad?" she asked quietly.

He slumped back against the wall of the cavern, and sighed deeply. "I don't know. They… they were kind of notorious around here when they were kids. After I came along, Daddy settled down but Hiram…" he rubbed his temple with the heel of his hand, "When Daddy died I spent some time in foster care. It was… It wasn't great. I thought when

Uncle Hiram agreed to take me in that it would be better. That it would all be better, but..." He fell into silence.

"I'm sorry," Mallory said, and reached up suddenly needing to feel the warmth of the sun. She put her hand in the jagged sliver of light that fell on the boulder. "I thought that you had... when you... I thought you might be working with them."

"I know," Hoodoo said. "And I'm sorry about that. I didn't have time to explain, Justin was... I just wanted to... protect you from him."

Mallory absently brushed at the thick layer of dust and sand that covered the boulder, unsure of what to say next. Something caught the light and glittered faintly. She focused on it and brushed at the sand a little more vigorously. She quickly cleared an area of the egg. It had a lumpy brown surface that looked like bubble gum that had been chewed by a giant. She moved her hand in a wide arc sweeping away the dust where the light from outside fell.

"What is it?" Hoodoo said, noticing that her attention had become focused on the stone.

"Wait," she breathed, "wait." A last brush of her hand cleared the spot beneath the light. Suddenly the entire egg glimmered into life, the refracted light filling it. Hoodoo pulled a handkerchief from his pocket and joined her, knocking away the century of fallen sand and dust that covered the egg. The more he removed, the more brilliant the light became. A diffuse glow filled the room with pinpricks of colored light splashing out of the giant egg like a disco ball. Embedded in the pitted surface of the stone were crystals, deep golden yellow, chartreuse, and grass green. There were thousands of them, ranging from the size of a pea to the size of a plum. Hoodoo reached out and ran a thumb over one of the crystals.

"It's real. The Frenchman's treasure. It's real," he breathed.

"It's not exactly gold..." Mallory said.

"Is... are these... diamonds?" he said, awe in his voice.

"No," she said. "I... I think it's olivine. I think this is a meteorite!"

Hoodoo whistled, long and low, the sound of awed appreciation. "How did it get here?"

"From the sky. From space. There's a meteorite blast field in Arizona that has some pieces like this... but nothing so... big." Mallory laughed hysterically. "It's probably been here millions of years. The better question is how did Tevbaugh find it?"

"How'd he do any of this? He blazed a trail through the heart of a mountain!" Hoodoo said. They both absently circled the meteorite, their fingers trailing over the surface as they walked as if reassuring themselves that it was real. The twinkling shafts of light that radiated from the stone played across both their faces filling the moment with magic.

"Your daddy came really close," Mallory said.

"I wonder what he would have made of this." Hoodoo said. "It's not what he thought it was."

"I doubt it's what anyone thought it was. Between this and the Sistine Chapel on the other side... this mesa's about to get a lot of scientific attention," she said.

"Sistine Chapel?" he started to say. "The big dome of petroglyphs? I wondered what you'd make of that."

He stopped abruptly. He turned his head toward the entrance with a strained look on his face. "Do you hear that?"

"What?"

"Helicopter," he said. "Helicopter!" and he ducked out of the cavern.

CHAPTER SIXTEEN

Mallory chased Hoodoo through the trees, both waving their arms as best they could and screaming fruitlessly. The sound of the helicopter filled the area, but they couldn't see it.

"They're searching the top of the mesa," Hoodoo yelled. "It won't take them long. We need to signal them!" He growled in frustration, "There's too many trees!"

"Can we... get up there?"

"I'm in no shape to climb," he said, exasperated. "It would take too long anyway. We need... smoke. Fire! We need to start a fire." He started pulling brush to a clear area.

"I have matches," she called and ran for her pack. She carefully lifted Justin's leg off the pack, and he groaned. "Sorry!" she said, feeling guilty that she had hurt him so badly. "Help is on the way. You're going to be okay."

She pulled items from her pack frantically, searching for her own emergency kit that she knew had a candle and matches inside. Her iPad slid out followed by her collection of cables and electronics. A glimmer of an idea began to form in her mind.

"Here!" she called, tossing the candle and matchbox to Hoodoo and then sprinted for the cabin. Leaning against the side was the drone. She flipped it over and snatched the battery from beside it. She pushed at the battery, trying to get it into the cavity, but it seemed too large or misshapen. With a shove and a grunt, she finally lodged it into the body of the drone.

She sprinted back to the pack snatching up her iPad, the zipper pack of electronics, and the rest of her survival kit.

"Please work. Please work. Please work," she chanted to herself as she ran back to the cabin.

Hoodoo had a small blaze going and was feeding it leaves and small twigs. "C'mon! C'mon!" he called, trying to encourage the fire. He kept stealing glances up to the sky, trying to catch a glimpse of the helicopter.

Mallory fell to her knees beside the drone and frantically dug in the survival kit. "Yes!" She cried and pulled the tiny emergency-sized roll of duct tape from the survival pack and strapped the tape across the battery, replacing the missing battery hatch cover. She flipped the unit over and pressed the power switch. Beside it, four tiny USB lights illuminated on the side: three red, one green. She winced; it didn't have much of a charge. From the corner of her eye, she caught the playing card-sized signal mirror. She grabbed that and a piece of paracord, knotting it to the drone as well. Maybe it would glitter in the sunlight and catch the helicopter pilot's eye. Now to see if she could pair the drone with her iPad. She groaned when the iPad booted, and she saw that it had only 4% power. "Okay. We can do this. Just have to work fast." She swiped past dozens of icons until she found the folder of drone control apps that she had installed during her time on the dig in Arizona and tapped the appropriate one.

This model of drone used a local Wi-Fi connection. She spotted the Wi-Fi network, the only one available, and tapped. Her heart sank when it requested a password.

She cursed under her breath and tried the default passwords that most systems used. It wasn't "password," and it wasn't "admin." The password for the unit at Toller's dig had been "link." Was that the default, or had they changed it? She tried it and was surprised to see that it was accepted.

"Yes!" she cheered, and pumped her fist. She tapped at the "launch" button on the iPad. Two of the four rotors sprang to life. She flicked at one with her finger and watched as it whirred into life as well. She tapped and flicked at the fourth, but no amount of cajoling seemed enough to wake it.

"C'mon. C'mon," she muttered and thumped the prop again. It whirred, and the entire unit rose to about five feet off the ground.

"Now let's see if we have enough power to get their attention," she muttered and pushed her finger upward on the screen. The drone drifted up as well, mirror dangling from beneath it. Mallory burst with a wild laugh. "Toller... I'm still taking you down, but if this saves my life..." She tilted the iPad, maneuvering between the large trees as the drone lifted. It drifted a bit to one side, probably the side with the bum rotor she guessed, but she thought she could compensate for it. She could see the ground through the downward facing camera on the drone, but the window that should have showed the forward facing camera was black. It didn't matter. "Hahahahahaha!" she cackled as it lifted up.

Hoodoo looked up from his fire, "What is that?" he called.

"Rich guy's drone!" she called back over the whir of the tiny propellers.

"How did you..." he said, jogging to her side.

"See if you can pull that branch aside," she said pointing at an errant tree that she was having trouble maneuvering around. He ran to it and leapt hanging from the branch for a moment as the drone slipped through the now open space and up toward the sky. The tiny signal mirror flashed in the light.

"Go, go, go!" she whispered and watched the drone slip past the edge of the sandstone wall that surrounded them. She glanced at the iPad and watched herself diminish in the camera.

"Can they see it?" Hoodoo called. The sound of the helicopter was faint, a low thrum.

"I don't know," she said, trying to keep the desperation out of her voice. "Please, please," she prayed. In the camera, she could see the top of the mesa and the deep cylindrical space that she was standing in.

"What's the range?" Hoodoo asked.

"Far enough," she responded. "I hope." Suddenly, the little drone began smoking and a thick plume of white smoke filled the air around it.

"What's happening?" Hoodoo asked, frantic.

"Dunno," she replied. There was a soft bursting noise like the pop of a distant balloon, and the screen in her hand went black. In the sky, there was a ball of yellow flame dropping rapidly. It fell beyond the rim of the canyon and disappeared. Mallory's heart fell with it. "The battery," she said. "I think the battery was damaged."

"They saw that!" he said. "They had to! They just had to." They both stared at the circle of sky above them counting the long seconds and watching the thin cloud of smoke from the battery fire fade away.

The little canyon filled with the booming thump of helicopter blades as the chopper swung into view above them and hovered in the center of the circle of sky. A small, fluorescent yellow clad figure hung from the side waving. Hoodoo stepped into a clearing returning the wave. Mallory's face was wet with streaming tears. The helicopter banked to the side and disappeared.

Hoodoo loped back to Mallory scooping her up by the waist and swinging her around. His laughter filled the air. "You did it!"

"Careful!" she called through her tears. "Ribs!"

He lowered her to her feet. "Sorry! I just... you did it!"

"Yeah. Yeah!" she said, and hugged him.

* * *

Mallory walked down the gleaming corridor of the hospital trying to keep her voice low as she chatted into her cellphone.

"Yes, Dr. Pickens, I understand," she said. "Yes, sir. I'll be there, sir. I will sir, I promise. First thing." She stopped in front of Hoodoo's room. He was chatting animatedly with Lynn, a large aluminum nose mask and wads of bandage taped to his face with medical tape. "Yes, sir. Thank you for this opportunity, sir. I promise you'll understand it all. Thank you. Goodbye," she took a deep breath and tapped the screen of the phone to disconnect. The shattered glass of the screen distorted the icons, but the phone seemed to work fine. The bandage on her hand caught in one of the cracks, and she pulled a bit to free it, leaving a strand of cotton imbedded in the phone.

At least she knew that the photos of the sherd she had found were safe. The first thing she had done once she had data coverage was sync them to the cloud.

It had taken nearly 6 hours to get all of them out of the Frenchman's Eye. Lifting the injured Justin and the under arrest Hiram out of the Eye required specialized equipment and handling. Hiram especially proved to be difficult since the Deputy with the rescue crew insisted that Hiram be handcuffed the whole time. Everyone was eventually delivered to a medical facility where Mallory was treated for dehydration, exposure, and a long list of bruises, scrapes, and injuries including a broken rib. All of this sent her mother into fits and Mallory could only assume that some benevolent god had interceded on her behalf to prevent her mother from actually coming to Utah.

"Mallory! Get in here," Hoodoo called. "Did you make a deal with your professors?"

"I'm meeting one of them next week at the South Pecos Conference," she said. "It's this annual gathering. All the archaeologists that have been working in the area for the summer will be there to discuss findings. I'm sure Toller will be there. Knowing him, he scheduled his entire dig to end just in time. He'll probably be the keynote." She settled into a chair beside his bed. "If I can prove my case, they are willing to work with me."

"Awesome!" Hoodoo said and beamed at her. "Did you find it? Your one right thing?"

"I think I did, yeah," she smiled. "How are things here?"

"He's good," Lynn said, and shook his arm. "They are probably releasing him tomorrow. A little dehydration won't keep him down long."

"My kidney's were failing, honey. I wouldn't call it 'little' dehydration..." he said. "But I'm bouncing back."

"What about Justin? The nurses won't tell me much," she asked.

"He'll be fine. He has a concussion, and he broke his arm. He'll be joining his dad in the county jail as soon as he's able," Hoodoo said.

"They officially arrested Hiram?"

"Yesterday. Deputy Reyes collected him straight out of his hospital bed. Terroristic threats, attempted murder, stalking, theft, destruction of government property... whatever else they could think of," Lynn said.

"There's one thing I don't get," Mallory said. "How did all of this start? How did Hiram know I found the map?"

"He watched you," Hoodoo said. "He told me all about it while we were chasing you. Him and Daddy'd had theories about that canyon for years. Hiram's been living pretty desperate for a while now, so I guess he really wanted to get his hands on that gold. He was camped above the canyon and saw you go in. He followed you from above. He watched you the whole time you were in there."

Mallory shivered to think that the evil man had been so close to her and she'd never realized it. "Why didn't you tell me about your dad? You said you didn't know of any connection between Tevbaugh and that canyon."

"I didn't think there was," he shrugged, and his IV line bounced. "It was a theory that Daddy and Hiram had, that it was the best water source between the town and the mesa. They figured the Frenchman would have stopped there to water his horse, but they scoured all of those canyons and never found anything."

"Leave it to a geocacher," Mallory laughed. "We know all the best hiding spots." She looked over her shoulder at the open door, and dropped her voice to a neat whisper. "And you're okay keeping what we found secret for just a bit?"

"Yeah," he said, matching her tone. "Go take care of your business with Toller. When you get back, you can announce that you've found the largest collection of petroglyphs in America, and I'll announce that I've found the largest pallasite meteorite. You know... I did some checking. Meteorites like that sell for about $10 a gram. A gram! Even if that thing only weighs a ton that's nearly 10 million dollars and I think it's a lot bigger than a ton."

"And how do you propose we get a rock that weighs a ton or more out of a 300 foot hole?" Lynn said. "Besides, it's BLM land. Technically the government owns that rock."

"It belongs in a museum anyway," Mallory added. "Maybe they'll name it after you. The Estes Meteorite."

"The Tevbaugh-Estes Meteorite," he said.

"Perfect," she smiled.

"Mallory..." Hoodoo started.

"Stop," she said. "You apologized enough. You had reasons for wanting to go in there, and I had reasons to follow you. Neither of us could have known about Hiram and Justin."

"I know. But they're my family. As ludicrous as it sounds I feel... responsible. I should have told you more."

"And I should have told you that I was essentially looking for place to hide," she shrugged. "It all comes out in the wash. You just need to get better. When I get back from the conference, I'm going to need to go back to the Eye and document those petroglyphs."

"And the meteorite," he added.

"And the meteorite," she agreed. "I'll need the best guide in Memphis." She placed her hand over his and squeezed.

"The best guide in Memphis?" Lynn quipped, grinning at them both. "I'll have to see if I'm available, but I'm sure we can work something out."

* * *

Dr. Jonathan Toller strolled onto the stage at the South Pecos Conference and accepted the applause that he knew was his due. He scanned the audience, looking specifically for the faces of a few colleagues and rivals whose academic body of work he was about to destroy with his findings from the Kaibab Reservation Dig. When his speech was over, he knew that not only would he have cemented his place in the archaeological pantheon, but he would also have shredded the work of a half dozen other people, most of them in the audience. He really hoped that at least one of them left the tent in tears.

"... Dr. Jonathan Toller!" the man introducing him finished. Toller tried for a second to remember the man's name, then decided that he didn't care. He shook the man's hand, muttered a thank you and assumed his position behind the podium. The first slide of his presentation appeared behind him.

"Ladies and gentlemen, esteemed colleagues, thank you for your attention today," he said, voice clear and strong with his signature charm. He reached up and smoothed his hair, *have to look good in the photos*, he thought. "I know that it's unusual for a presentation at the Conference to last for longer than 15 minutes, and I beg your indulgence. I believe the information that I have to present here today will change how we view archaeology in the Southwest forever..."

He continued to drone as Mallory slipped into the last row of the tent and maneuvered to a space beside her mentor, Matthew Pickens. "Dr. Pickens," she whispered by way of greeting.

"Campbell," he said, deep voice rumbling even at a whisper, "are you sure about this?"

"Yes," she said, trying to sound more sure than she felt, "absolutely. One right thing."

Ignoring the cryptic remark, he said, "Okay. Let's hope this doesn't burn us both."

From the podium Toller intoned, "I am prepared to present undeniable evidence that the originating culture of the Kayenta Valley Region was the Virgin Anasazi," he paused for a dramatic breath, "NOT the Kayenta Anasazi as previously thought by many of our... colleagues." He said the word 'colleagues' as if he were referring to the mules that hauled rock on his dig sites.

There were a few murmurs in the audience. This had been a hotly debated topic for decades. A few people who had only been cursorily paying attention sat up straighter and shifted a bit in their seats.

"If you'll turn your attention to the first slide..." he began again after a suitably long pause.

"Excuse me, Dr. Toller?" Came a voice from the back of the room.

Toller rolled his eyes, exasperated at the interruption. "Please wait until my presentation is complete before..."

"I'm sorry, I just wanted to know if your presentation would be accounting for the contradictory evidence found by my student."

"I'm sorry. Who are you?" Toller demanded. He squinted into the audience, trying to see exactly who was speaking. A number of faces in the audience turned towards Dr. Pickens.

"Oh, Matthew Pickens, UNC."

"Well, Mr. Pickens, if you'd allow me..."

"Doctor."

"What?" said Toller, charm cracking and his frustration beginning to show. Every head in the audience was now ping-ponging between the two men.

"It's *Doctor* Pickens."

"Yes, I'm sure, if you would just..."

"What he's trying to ask is why you are presenting a paper here when there is conflicting evidence at the site. Evidence that *I* found and that you swept under the carpet." Mallory strode down the central aisle of the tent, voice loud and strong. The attention of the whole room was on her. "Joyce?" she said. The small woman stood up from her seat on the outer aisle and pulled a sheet from a second projector. On the opposing wall, a photo of Mallory in her unit at the Kaibab Reservation site blossomed into view. Joyce clicked a button on a remote, and the slide changed to a photo of the sherd she had found, in situ, measuring tools and photo cards surrounding it.

"What is this?" Toller demanded, a break in his voice.

"This is Ka72-3-29. A piece of Kayenta pottery, found on your dig, below... uhm..." She snatched an abstract from the hands of a nearby audience member and flipped to the references at the back of the paper, "below Ka76-6-11 which you seem to have highlighted in your paper as the smoking gun for your thesis."

"Can someone please get this girl--" Toller began.

From the back of the room, Dr. Pickens' voice cut through the uproar. "Will your presentation be taking this evidence into account?"

The room was filled with the sound of pages flipping as the audience more closely examined the abstract that they had been given. Murmurs began on one side and were soon spreading across the audience.

"Excuse me, Miss...?" said a white haired woman with deeply tanned skin. Her voice hushed the audience, most of whom looked at her in deference. A few faces even carried awe at her sudden appearance.

"Campbell," said Dr. Pickens. "Her name is Mallory Campbell."

"Miss Campbell, are you suggesting that Dr. Toller has... disregarded... certain pieces of data in his thesis?" the white haired woman asked.

"I'm suggesting..." Mallory paused and reconsidered, "No, I'm saying. I'm saying... that he may have outright destroyed artifacts that didn't support his thesis," she said.

The room erupted in noise as people began asking questions and demanding Toller's response. The white haired woman climbed on stage and raised her hands over the audience silently commanding their attention and respect. The audience slowly came to silence.

"Ladies and gentlemen, I believe we should adjourn for the afternoon," intoned the white haired woman. "Dr. Toller, Dr. Pickens, Ms. Campbell, if you'll come with me please."

"Excuse me! I will not be..." sputtered Toller his face turning red.

The woman held up a hand and he stopped midsentence. "I assure you, you *will* have your turn to speak," she said.

"But…"

"Later," she said simply and turned away from Toller. He looked around expecting his assistants and acolytes to be gathered behind him as they always were. Instead, he found himself on an empty stage.

"Ms. Campbell, if you would," the older lady said.

"And Joyce!" Mallory said motioning to the girl at the back of the tent.

"Ah… yes, of course. Please, join us, uh… Joyce."

They all silently followed the diminutive woman across an open stretch of grass. She settled on the bench of a picnic table and indicated that they should join her. "I assume you all know who I am?" she asked.

"Dr. Betsy Carder, the South Pecos Conference director," Dr. Pickens said, saving Mallory the embarrassment.

"Correct," she said. "I'll admit that I don't really have any power in this situation. I'm not on the board of Jonathan's university nor am I the arbiter of how research should be conducted in this region, but I do have a… bit of pull," she rocked her hand slightly in a 'so-so' gesture.

"Wait just a minute!" Toller commanded, the red returning to his face.

"Jonathan. Do shut up," Dr. Carder said. "Now. Tell me your story Mallory."

It came in a gush, with Joyce adding details here and there, and Toller attempting to interject. Carder consistently shut him down and listened to Mallory's tale, asking clarifying questions when she needed to, and she looked at the photos that Mallory had in her phone. When Mallory was done, Dr. Carder folded her hands in her lap and turned to Toller.

"Jonathan, where is this sherd? Ka72-3-29?" she asked with a slow deliberateness.

"I'd… well, I'd have to check," he said. "You can hardly expect me to know the condition and whereabouts of every… minor… sherd found on my site. Besides, I don't believe there ever was a unit with that designation on this site."

"I see," Carder said. She looked around at the assembled group, looking each of them in the eye, then scrolled through the photos again. She wrapped a knuckle on the wood of the picnic table, just once, a gavel to the end of her deliberations. "Well. Jonathan, as a… personal favor to me… I would very much like you to look into that." She said it with no malice.

She sounded like nothing more than a kindly old lady asking a neighbor to check on her plants or mow her lawn. "These photos of Ms. Campbell's are very clear. I'm sure she'd be happy to provide you with copies. I'd like you to go through your sherds and find the one that matches it. If you can't produce the sherd... well... As I said, I have no authority over you, but you may find it a bit more... difficult... to get permits for your digs in this region in the future. I have quite a few friends in this area, I believe you'll find."

"You... you have no right!" Toller spluttered.

"Jonathan. I'm asking for a favor from someone I'd like to consider a friend. You may do me that favor, or you may not. It's up to you."

Toller stood, his face a blank. "I'll look into it," he said flatly, and stalked away without another word.

Betsy Carder turned to Mallory. A long moment passed between them. "Ms. Campbell, have you chosen your thesis yet?" She said it with a calm, pleasant voice, Toller seemingly forgotten.

Mallory looked at Dr. Pickens then back to her. "I... recently made that decision, yes. I haven't told Dr. Pickens about it yet..."

"Well. I'm sure whatever it is it will be very interesting. I'd be honored to act as one of your advisors when the time comes," Dr. Carder said. "Especially if it involves returning to this area for the field work." She smiled genially. "We need a few more women in science like you."

Mallory returned the smile, and glancing at Dr. Pickens said, "Have you ever heard of the Lost Frenchman?"

A NOTE FROM THE AUTHOR

Thank you for coming on this adventure with me! *The Lost Frenchman* came to me as an almost fully formed idea while on a hike in the Bryce Canyon National Park and, by the end of that hike, I had most of the story outlined in my mind. Like the best geocaching adventures I began the story of Hoodoo and Mallory (and Jean Tevbaugh!) thinking I was going to find one thing, but found myself lost a few times and, in the end, arrived at the destination by a different path than I had originally thought. I'm thrilled by what I discovered along the way, and I hope you are too.

Almost all of the locations described in the story are based on real locations that I visited while on several vacations to southern Utah. Paradise Mesa is based on the mesa called "Chesler Park" in the Canyonlands National Park Needles District (38° 06.592'N 109° 51.087'W). The Needles District is less visited than the Islands In The Sky District to the north but, in my opinion, is the more interesting area of the park. The Chesler Park hike at Needles is hands-down the best hike I have ever taken (even though there are no geocaches on it since it is a National Park). The constantly changing scenery and challenging terrain really make it a carnival ride of a hike. Have a look at the coordinates in Google Earth and check out some of the many photographs that are posted in the area and, if you ever find yourself in the area, skip the more curated Islands in the Sky section of Canyonlands and make the drive down to Needles. It's well worth it. The "Joint Trail" portion of the Chesler Park hike (38° 6.144'N 109° 51.542'W) inspired the deep, cracked stones where Mallory and Hoodoo first become separated in Chapter 9. A great example of the "fins" formation can be seen at 38° 47.864'N 109° 36.619'W in Arches National Park. The "Frenchman's Eye" is based on the Lower Calf Creek Falls which can be found at 37° 49.720'N 111° 25.142'W.

The Frenchman himself was inspired by the story of Jacob Waltz known as "The Dutchman," a local legend in Northern Arizona. The Dutchman didn't leave any rosaries or quartz lantern shields, but he left some peculiar maps behind and people have been looking for his treasure ever since. It is estimated that more than 8,000 people a year make the pilgrimage into the Superstition Mountains seeking Waltz's treasure.

The Mormon War and the Cotton Mission are real history, though there's no evidence that anyone from Egypt (or Algeria) came to give them tips on growing cotton.

The Frenchman's ultimate treasure was based on the Fukang Pallasite which, even though it was found in China, has found a home at the University of Arizona. Many similar (though much smaller) meteorites have been found in the Southwest.

I'd like to take a moment to thank the people who read early drafts of this novella, Heather Uebel, Mark Saunders, Sandy Portacio, Brett Rogers and Amy Smith. Thanks to Audrey Dawson for making sure I got my archaeology right, Anjeanette Stokes and Loretta Grace for being my Catholicism resources, Jeremy Jacobowitz for being my police resource, and the members of r/drones for helping me with information about drones. Enormous thanks to Wendy Martling, who provided story feedback, editing services, and generally encouraged me to keep at it.

ALSO BY CULLY LONG

HOW TO PUZZLE CACHE
LESSONS, TIPS, TRICKS, and HINTS FOR SOLVING GEOCACHE PUZZLES

by CULLY LONG
FOREWORD by SONNY and SANDY PORTACIO

FACED WITH A MAP FULL OF BLUE QUESTION MARKS AND NO IDEA WHERE TO START?

Geocaching novices and pros alike are often daunted by puzzle and mystery caches. Ciphers, enigmatic photos, nonsensical text, or just a blank page, it often isn't clear what the CO wants or expects you to do, and even less clear how any of it will lead you to a cache.

THIS BOOK WILL HELP YOU ASK -- AND ANSWER -- ALL THE RIGHT QUESTIONS.

Over 300 pages of lessons, tips, tricks and hints for dealing with even the trickiest puzzle caches. Step-by-step techniques that start with examining the cache page and lead you through codes, ciphers, steganography, math, music, and dozens of other common puzzle cache types.

Paperback available at Lulu.com, or Amazon.com.
Spiral bound edition available at Lulu.com.

For more information please visit HowToPuzzleCache.com.

Sean loves geocaching and wants to share it with his friends! Follow them on their adventure with exciting coloring pages, and rewarding activity pages that also teach geocaching basics and good geocache stewardship.

With art by Cully Long, and activities created in conjunction with Sandy Portacio of the Podcacher Podcast, "Sean and Friends" provides a welcome activity for geo-kids who might be trapped indoors by weather or other circumstance, as well as a way to introduce muggle-kids to the basics of caching.

Paperback available at Lulu.com, or Amazon.com.

www.ingramcontent.com/pod-product-compliance
Lightning Source LLC
Chambersburg PA
CBHW020433180626
46812CB00003B/1209